The Jackal Awake

David Patrick Beavers was bo tiny California town in coa earned his BA in Drama fro California and his MFA in scriptwriting University. While he currently lives in Los Angeles where he works on projects for film and theatre, he entertains notions of chucking it all and escaping to the timeless streets of New Orleans. His first novel, *Jackal in the Dark*, is also published by Millivres Books International.

The Jackal Awakens

David Patrick Beavers

Millivres Books International
Brighton

First Published in 1995 by Millivres Books (Publishers)
33 Bristol Gardens, Brighton BN2 5JR, East Sussex, England

A CIP catalogue record for this book is available from the British Library

ISBN 1 873741 22 7

Typeset by Hailsham Typesetting Services, 4-5 Wentworth House, George Street, Hailsham, East Sussex BN27 1AD

Printed and bound by Biddles Ltd., Walnut Tree House, Woodbridge Park, Guildford, Surrey GU1 1DA

Distributed in the United Kingdom and Western Europe by Turnaround Distribution Co-Op Ltd., 27 Horsell Road, London N5 1XL

Distributed in the United States of America by InBook, 140 Commerce Street, East Haven, Connecticut 06512, USA

Distributed in Australia by Stilone Pty Ltd, PO Box 155, Broadway, NSW 2007, Australia.

My sincerest thanks to Sebastian Beaumont and Peter Burton

To David Richey, Kiki Hall, Spencer Beglarian, Laura Toffler, Clemi Boubli, Grant Neumann, Tracy Barone and my favourite cousin, Tiffany Welch, for all their unwaivering support

To Rex, John and Steve

And to everyone seeking a new beginning

This book is dedicated to one most cherished friend who has walked the path with me. To Carron V. Leon with my deepest affection

The humidity clung to the concrete of the sidewalk and the brick work of the buildings around me, transforming the city into a vast, stinging haze. Blacktop oozed tar. Petroleum derivatives perfumed the body by way of diesel fumes and oil leaks from untended cars. Living in the impressionist's nightmare, I thought, as I made my way down the narrow walk, careful to avoid excretions and vomit and the worst of all – gum. All forms of flypaper to snare the unaware worker ants called pedestrians. An open spigot of salty sweat cascaded down from the crest of my head, down, stinging eyes, down, to bathe the razor blade abrasion on my chin, still on down these tributaries of sweat ran to soak my shirt through. Sweat poured freely. I hoped to God this wouldn't bring on another case of jock itch. It was 101 degrees with a hundred percent humidity. I itch in the heat. I'm rabid in humidity. My ears buzzed like a power line, drowning out the horns of the cars that bleated like sheep caught in quicksand. Gridlock was deadlock. Better the drivers beat their car horns than each other, I thought. Maybe not. Carrion to cadavers, the city was in imbalance. God, where's the rainmaker's magic.

It was locked away on a movie set somewhere in Los Angeles where gallon upon gallon of water would be wasted for take upon take of a woman washing her luxurious locks in a desert thunder storm tempered by soothing indigo back lights. All this in the name of promoting yet another shampoo of promise. What promise? That your hair won't be stripped to brittle clean? That your hair won't look like you washed it with greasy mutton fat? How would such a shampoo work on my sweat drenched hair at this moment? Sudsy suds would in time rinse clean away with another outpouring of body fluid.

I rounded the corner and slapped a palm against the cast iron gate. Flecks of black enamel paint seared into my flesh as I forced its rusted hinges to give way and open to let me in. I brushed my palm against my jeans feeling the dampness invading my crotch. Jock itch to a man is like a yeast infection to a woman. As persistent as fleas and twice as annoying. I tried not to scratch as I walked up to the stoop where Peter and Paul were lounging on the steps, stripped down to threadbare Speedos and frying themselves under the ultraviolet broiler. As I stepped past them, Paul caught my shin and pulled me back.

He leaned his pretty head back and pursed his lips in a mock smile. "Do you have any oil?"

"Vinegar and piss, babe. That's all I have." I tried to move on. His grip held. "What? You really want oil?"

"Sit."

Peter cocked his head my way, grinning. "He wants a cigarette."

"You quit smoking," I said.

"I quit buying them, not smoking them."

I pulled the damp pack from my shirt pocket and dropped it in his lap. He fished around the opening, trying to pull one out.

"They're clumped together," he said.

"It's humid. They're moist. You want fresh and dry, go buy a pack yourself," said Peter as he stood up and stretched. The faded orange material of his swimsuit clung to his ass cheeks like Veronica's veil to the Christ's face. A truly holy image. He turned toward us, gently tugging the material, loosening it about his crotch. "Whaddaya think?" he asked.

"About what?" said Paul as he tossed me back the cigarettes and mimed for a light. I sat down and lit his cigarette, garnering a cursory nod of thanks.

"Am I tan enough?"

Paul flopped back on the step, inclined on bent elbows, each padded by a stack of magazines. I lit a cigarette. Studied Peter's form. Behind him, passers-by padded along, scarcely giving notice, preoccupied with seeing beyond the stinging haze of hot, heavy, wet air. Peter looked too comfortable standing there near naked, his skin glistening slightly as his pores strained to work, while the backdrop of the city's civilised grunted as they gamboled along, loosening ties, carrying sport coats, tugging at suffocating pantyhose welded to skin and lugging their daily lives with them in purses, gym bags, briefcases, backpacks and sacks.

"You're uneven," Paul said.

"Screw it," he said as he picked up his butt crushed towel and wiped himself down. "Like, I gotta have a yard. Some place to spread out and do it right. This city's a fuckin' scow." He balled up the towel and parked himself back on it on the step, reaching over to snag the pack of smokes from my pocket. I flipped him the lighter. "You," he said to me, "You got the right idea. Stay in your jeans. Stay dressed. Block the UV's 'cause you're only gonna be pale again come November."

I snorted a plume of smoke, caught the pack and lighter he flipped back to me and adjusted the wallet that was pressing into my buttock. "It's New York. People like us aren't supposed to be comfortably stretching out on aqua chaise lounges like we're living a Club Med ad."

"What bored up your butt?" said Paul.

"Boredom," I said.

"New York. You're bored. There's an error in your equation," said Paul.

"Wanna go catch a movie?" asked Peter. "At least it'll be air conditioned."

"We're broke," Paul said.

We sat there, smoking, letting sweat drip down our faces and forms, staring idly ahead as people shuffled to and fro on St.Mark's. The building was an old five floor walk up, built by German immigrants before they left the East Village area not long after the *General Slocum* fire. The *General Slocum* was a pleasure steamer that sailed on the East River up to the Bronx shoreline. It caught fire on a trip, killing most of the children of Germantown who were on an excursion, or so I'd heard. Still the building stood with its railroad or shotgun type apartments. Living room into kitchen into tub room into toilet. The tub rooms used to be whispers of a bedroom back in the days when people bathed in washtubs in the kitchen. Somewhere in the twenties they got converted into the masterpieces of nightmarish plumbing they are today. Claw tubs with rusting spigots. Oval shower curtain rods mysteriously fastened to the walls. Four flats on each floor sharing hot water from one dinky water heater. I'd helped Paul and Peter redo their flat. We'd chipped, scraped and sanded away a millennium of paint on the woodwork only to find mismatched woods underneath. White pine casements, oak sashes and, strangely, redwood sills. Underneath layer upon layer of ripped up linoleum we found the sole source of insulation, newspapers from 1912. Beneath that, subflooring. Peter laid down half-inch plywood, padding and carpet. The carpet, the new paint, the new fixtures made their apartment more inviting to the eye, but did little to combat the drafty cold of winter or the suffocating heat of the summer.

"Wanna go sit on the fire escape and chew ice?" said Peter.

"I want a pool," Paul said.

I arose from the concrete block that numbed my ass, "I am going to go sit in a tanker full of ice."

"Why? You just get out and start sweating again," said Paul.

"Maybe by the time I get out it'll be night," I said as I entered the building. My boots seemed to clomp-squish as I ascended the stairs. At each floor the sweltering air seemed to get hotter and wetter, hanging thick like mucous in congested lungs. I was walking through a fifth floor cloud, feeling my way to my door. Key's jangled. Entry. The room, the main room, the only real room, closed in about me as I shut myself in. Like being enclosed in a vacuum tube. I felt nauseated. In the kitchen, I peeled away the layers of constricting clothing, letting my naked pores breathe as best they could. I opened up the freezer to lap up a chilly blast. Stale air assailed my nostrils. The freezer was failing from age, from fighting the insufferable temperature inside this flat. There was no ice for an ice bath. Typical, I thought. Even machines were losing the battle. I went into the tub room, drew a bath full of lukewarm cold water and stepped in to immerse myself in wetness.

Quiet seeped into my subconscious as my eyelids, lazy with a fatigue, lowered slowly to a lash obscured slit of sight. Feather-like patterns seemed to drift by, ghosts of imagined spirits having no name, no place to attach themselves to. Down went the shades. Darkness penetrated by whispers of light. Residue. The shadows persisted. Images floated and interlocked like playing cards shuffled in a casino dealer's hands. I could hear the echoing drip-drip-drip of drops seeking their escape from the faucet rumbling through the cooling bath as I sank deeper into relaxation. That dull, soothing sound generated by the water's pressure upon my eardrum, coupled with the steady tympanic beating – internal rhythms – whispered questions. Is there light at the centre of time? Is there time? The fleeting form of a dragon fell into a slot of the mental slide carousel, halting the dizzying movements. A kindly dragon, looking so very sad and alone. Puff, perhaps? That mighty mythical dragon of folk song fame, now fallen – crestfallen. Pain bled through his abandoned eyes, as devoid of spirit as a dead man's gaze. Hollow black eyes that had long ago cried themselves dry. A hunger was left. A hunger ravenous for simple acknowledgement, a few high spirited, entreating words. I watched him. He returned my stare, desperately wanting me to engage him. To help him find that spirit of youth and purpose stolen from him by a willful, selfish child who'd turned his back on him so many seasons ago. But, I'd forgotten the game, the magical words, the purpose of youthful spirit. He stared a moment more, then with a heavy sigh, he lowered that majestic head. His pleading eyes, downcast. Suddenly his head cocked, away from me. I strained to listen. Far off in another time, the gleeful laughter of children drift over, around, through barriers real and imagined, calling his name. That noble head rose high up into the air. Those cracked, dry nostrils sniffed the call upon the winds. Here was his entreaty. Slowly this shrunken hulk arose from his bed, his stiff joints filling with youthful elasticity. Grayed pavis hide gave way as his brilliant green scales filled his form with strength and vitality. The call of the young flooded around him, sweeping him up on a wave of euphoria. He turned to me one last time. Moist emerald nostrils glistened as they flared with new found life. And those eyes. Large, shimmering orbs of liquid night once again ablaze with star fire and oh the possibilities that awaited. He shed one tear for me as his ember red wings stretched proudly to carry him off to a place, to a time beyond my reach. As he ascended the sky, that lone tear, of joy or of sorrow, fell like a snowflake that was on a lazy course to an unspecified region. Then a flurry of faces whizzed by like a blasting winter storm driven mercilessly by some violent, biting north winds. Faces of children. All children ever seen, riding that orbiting notion of time telling me that life is a hunger constantly needing to be sated. The flurry slowed to hazy silhouettes as I felt my chest expand and contract slightly with each slow breath. Silhouettes of then. The early years back home in Santa Cruz when my parents were younger than I'd ever imagined them to have been. So very young. Younger than I was now. Perhaps that time still exists somewhere locked into a circular orbit, waiting to be relived. Waiting to be rediscovered. The later years reached in like trellising vines seeking rooting. Images of Rex and Taylor and Sue and Jill. And Lisa. Lisa with the red, red roses. People from then, not now. Friends and loves of that turbulent time of life when chaos ruled the order for the day. Time gone by. Time never to be reclaimed save for some fluke of physical and natural law that might send me hurtling through a time warp in the guise of an errant black hole blown off its cosmic course. Some time in some future, perhaps, but not now. The thud-thud-thudding of the ballpeen striking a metal spike and ramming it into a lathe and plaster sheath knocked the now into my consciousness as I sat up with a splash to listen. For God's sake. Humming. Happy humming and hammering. The never-before and never-to-be seen superintendent of this old brownstone must have leased the vacant apartment behind me. Wham-thud. Wham-thud. Wham-thud. Three more nails into the aging walls of the coffin.

I stepped out of the tub and into that adjoining room with the loose commode and gnat-sized sink. I could hear the scraping of paintings or framed pictures being hung and straightened

on the other side of the wall. And humming. Definitely male humming. Off-key, annoying but happy humming. God, I hated humming. Peter and Paul beside me blaring their bizarre collections of alternate music and Julie behind them with her even more disturbing sounds of wood saws on aluminum pipe or wood saw with bow or wood saw on steel link chains. Wasn't the screeching of almost crime victims, the slurred barrage of obscenities from three a.m. drunks waddling home from the Waa-Waa Hut, the bleating car horns, the haranguing pitches from street vendors, the general vomiting of dysfunctional noises from the dysfunctional city spewing through the masonry and closed windows day in and day out enough? This new man must have been unaware that his pathetic, albeit happy, humming was going to have to bow and defer to the master sound mixer – the streets. The humming stopped. Silence. Then that voice boomed like a cannon shot through the wall.

"Did I crack your plaster?!" Naked and wet, I stood there staring at the wall. A girl I knew in Los Angeles had once been in a movie about a talking wall, but I didn't recall it being anything like this. "Hello?!" Knuckles rapped lightly on the wall. "Shave and a haircut" was the tune. Rap-rap. At least the ditty deserved a reply. I stepped back from the wall and snatched up a towel to maintain modesty from this Superman next door. "I'm John!" he bellowed. "I'll hammer later if you'd rather I wait!"

"No!" I bellowed back, wondering if this stranger was any kin to Little Abner. "Hammer away! I've got an appointment to keep!"

He yelled back an open invitation to drop by. I towelled myself off - a pointless venture – and slid into fresh underwear, shorts and a very faded red tank top that needed to be retired soon. An itch. I pulled up the leg of my shorts. No sign of a rash yet. Maybe prickly heat. I'd buy some ointment later down at the overpriced market on Second Avenue.

While thongs would have been more comfortable, I was loathe to leave my feet so vulnerable. Crew socks and one of the pair of alternating tennis shoes would be tolerable. Paul's one-rap knock was all he felt he needed to do for entry, into anyone's apartment. I often toyed with his conceptions of neighbourliness by securing the dead bolt on the door. This wasn't one of those times. He charged right on inexhaling a trail of smoke like some snuffed out dragon.

"Peter doesn't think I should wear this outside," he said as he posed. His threadbare black Speedo had transformed into a very slight, cobalt blue, lycra thong. Ass cheeks jiggled a bit as he turned toward the kitchen then fell headfirst into my refrigerator rummaging for something to eat.

"Apples in the crisper," I said.

He squared down, sorted methodically through the small red delicious apples that somehow managed to stay crisp and tart in this oven of an environment. He chomped into one,then closed up shop and faced me, his arms outstretched as he observed his own form.

"Well," he said.

"Unsightly tan lines," I said.

"They'll even out. Eventually."

"You're not going to Fire Island, Long Island, Ellis Island or any other island, so why worry?"

"You sound like Peter," he said as he swallowed half the apple with another bite.

"Who's the guy in 5B?"

"You met him?"

"Indirectly."

"His name's John Wilhelm or Vilhelm. From Boston or Barstow or Bennington or something like that."

"You'd make a good cop."

"He's kind of cute, in an odd way. Not my type, though," Paul said as he leaned out the window onto the fire escape. "Fuck'im. He just thinks I'm doing this to make him jealous."

"You're doing it because you've a beautiful body and you're vain," I said.

"So what if I am? I'm not getting any younger an' ripping these muscles to fuck and back again three hours a day every other day's not gonna last forever. I got a good package. Why not show it off?"

"Fine, Paul," I said. "You do what you want to do, but leave me out of the arguments, okay?"

"You always side with Peter. You know that?"

"Paul, if I had your body, I'd be showing it off, too." Paul looked a bit defeated. "What?" I asked. He just slumped on to the edge of my bed, staring and picking at some nonexistent hangnail.

"We haven't done it in eight months," he confessed. "He . . . he tested positive then. I just went back to the clinic last month. Still negative." I sat down beside him, pulling his resistant body into me, into a hug. Salty tears and saliva flowed freely as he let loose with great sobs of frustration, of anger, of ache, melding with our sweat. He released it all in the few slowly ticking minutes it took, then drew a deep, deep breathe and sighed. He pulled back, looking at me, but not looking at me. "What am I supposed to do? He won't do anything with me past a hug and a fucking peck on the lips. Go turn some fucking tricks 'til I pop up with a positive test, too? I hate this fucking shit," he said as he wearily flopped back on the bed.

"Well, I'm no sage," I said as I stretched out beside him. "We all know the psycho-babble responses. His problem. Your problem. Talk, explore options, meet half way, blah, blah, blah . . ."

"Talk, talk, talk," he laughed. "I've talked so much I'm windier than Chicago."

"It's your life. You stay, or, you go."

He gazed at me with those soft brown eyes. I felt somewhat like a parent or elder sibling as I brushed the strands of chestnut hair from his forehead. A slight hesitation, then he gently clasped my hand with his own and drew it down his face, pressing it softly against his chest. "You feel that?" he whispered. I could feel it. His heart. A steady, yet winsome beat . . . beat . . . "How," he continued, "How do I make him understand that I'm still alive?"

"Moonlight. Humidity. A bath."

"Been there. Did that," he said as he sat up. Vertebrae rippled as he arched forward, their spines pressing up through a low valley of muscle and flesh. I flashed for a moment to another time, to another back. The back of a young hustler, scarred by church key can opener. Taylor's back. That was then. I pulled up behind him. Massaged his shoulders, his neck. He reached up, took my hands and pulled me about him like a comfortable old sweater. Vulnerability makes vulnerability. I wanted to melt into him. Had wanted to do so for a very long time. But no. Lessons have been learned. I hugged him hard and kissed his temple.

"You love him," I said. "He does love you."

A smile cracked on his lips. "But I need to get fucked," he quipped. As he stood up, I slumped forward, belly flopping at the edge of the mattress. His full cheeks were a cigarette length away. I hungered. As he hungered. As the dragon had hungered. Paul turned and knelt before me at the foot of the bed. His sad eyes danced ever so slightly from side to side trying to gain access to what lay beyond my fixed gaze. "I need . . ." he whispered.

"Not me."

Crimson cheeks bulged with another great smile. He proffered a hand to help me rise above our subjective desires to plant my feet firmly on the floor. "Patience isn't easy, Paul. I know that very well. If you want to tan that glorious rear of yours, you're free to use my fire escape."

Bashful, somewhat guilty eyes nodded their thanks as I grabbed my keys and damp wallet. "Pete's always liked the look of me'n him. Maybe that's vain to say, but I like it."

"A mismatched match of bookends," I said as I opened the door. A handsome pair . . . Of what, I'm not sure."

Out in the hall we paused briefly before his door, exchanging a slight smile and a hug. Peter was so damned lucky, I thought. I could only hope that he'd put fears to rest and resume with his life with this man.

"Where're you headed off to?" he asked.

"No place," I said. "John Wilhelm-Vilhelm's busy jackhammering around the sweat box."

"Well, you're broke so don't go shopping." I shook my head and gave him a titty pinch. He flinched with a grin as we tossed good-byes.

*****

New York is a weird city. I'd come here for a change, for a graduate degree, for the frenetic energy, for the diversity, for the challenge. Once I'd finished my undergraduate degree in Los Angeles, I drifted for a time, moving from Los Angeles to Newport Beach to Santa Cruz to Fresno to Santa Cruz working at everything from managing a liquor store to being an insurance claim processor. My whole experience of living, per se, had been rooted in California. New York offered distance, separation from that entirety of myself. I had first come here on a visit. My friend, Carron V., had encouraged me to fly in. I had other friends in this city who'd migrated here once we were released from the penitentiaries of higher education. They all echoed Carron with encouragements of "give it a shot." Well, on that first trip, I hit Manhattan during a wonderfully airy Spring. Winter's frost still kept the air crisp in the morning while optimistic sunshine warmed my face in the afternoon. And the energy I felt . . . dizzying like speed without the delirium. Everything made me think. People were interesting. There was substance to conversations. There were performances, artshows, rinky-dink movie houses with the most obscure foreign films, coffee houses to retire to after any event to discuss and debate. And you didn't have to drive. This was particularly alluring. This city had a mass transportation system that was effective. So, my brief ten day jaunt here was enough to send me back home to Santa Cruz to retrieve my life and ship it all back to the city. Somewhere in that whirlwind of optimistic and opportunistic outlook, I'd failed to research the down side. The never ending noise, save for when the city was muffled with a thick blanket of snow from some unseasonal winter storm, the difficulties and expenses of 'flat' dwelling and the insufferable humidity that bore down in summer months. I walked in this haze now. Walked toward Washington Square.

I had no focus for this excursion. It was walking to walk. Usually, one had a need to have been someplace three hours prior, hence walking anywhere was more a matter of charging ahead, dodging other like minded bodies steering their own hurried courses. It seemed an almost unacceptable action, to walk the streets without a fixed destination in mind. I walked to observe. Everything seemed as it had always been. Cooper Square. The subway station. The large cube sculpture that pivoted when pushed that was somehow supposed to integrate humanity and art. The University buildings clumped here and there from Broadway to Sixth. The park. Splotchy patches of grass bordering asphalt and an inactive fountain. There was a drought. Even the pigeons and squirrels were more churlish and aggressive than ever, assaulting anyone who crossed their paths to give up any food or drink they had the misfortune of having in their possession. Sweating bodies were littered about melting like ice cream cones being nuked in a microwave oven at a very low setting. There had to be someplace to go to get away from this. There was no place to go that wouldn't be inundated with irritable humans and angry little animals. My crotch itched, giving me a purpose and a direction to walk.

*****

The pharmacy was old, probably having had its grand opening the day of Lincoln's inauguration. The pharmacist seemed just as old. He bagged up a tube of ointment. I paid him and left. No words were exchanged. As I stepped out on the street, I removed the tube from its carton, pitched the carton and bag in the trash and slid the ointment into my pocket. It was getting dark. Finally. With the ebb of evening came a cooling period. Not much of one, but enough to be noticeable. Perhaps John Wilhelm-Vilhelm had quieted down. I could open my windows, turn on electric fans and collapse to rest up for the following day. Sunday. Sunday then Monday and back to the ordinary existence of work. I was an Administrative Assistant's assistant at the University. I let out a sigh at the thought of routine and lit a damp cigarette.

"Do you have another one of those?" came the voice. I turned around. A young man with mussed, tawny hair, hazel eyes and genetically flawless features hopped off the hood of a parked car and approached me, offering the remaining half of his donut.

"Sure," I mumbled as I handed him a cigarette and the lighter. A rumpled white shirt, black jeans, black tennis shoes,a burgundy apron and a small gym bag slung over his shoulder made me think instantly that he was a waiter.

"You want some of my donut?" he said.

"Pass. Thanks anyway." I glanced to one side and caught a glimpse of DO-NUT DELIGHT with its sorry, stale looking baked goods sitting on gold, icing-flecked racks in the counter case. I doubted that even the flies would've chomped down on any of the remaining goods.

"They're pretty crappy," he said as he pitched the remainder of his meal into a trash can.

"Going to work or just getting off?" I asked.

"Off. I was out of town last week. Took the train in this morning and went straight to work."

"So why are you out here now, parked on your car and eating that hunk of lard and stale sugar?"

"Oh . . .," he said as he shifted back and forth on his feet, "I got locked out of my place and I've been trying to call this girl I know to see if I can crash with her for the night, but she's not home."

"Why not sit in the car? It'd be more comfortable."

"It's not mine. I just got tired of standing an' sat down." He glanced about absently. "Maybe I should try callin' her again." He fumbled in his pocket for some change, spilling a great many coins as he yanked his hand out. Money scramble. I helped him catch and collect it all.

"Waiter, huh?" I said.

"Yeah." He pointed to the beat up payphone on the street corner. "I'll just call . . ." He charged on ahead. I wasn't sure if I was supposed to follow him, but I did. He plunked in his quarter and dialled. I could hear the ringing on the other end, could hear the young woman's generic greeting and the ever irritating beep. "Emma? It's Jeremy again. I'm kinda still stuck. The fuckhead's still got me locked out an' isn't gonna bend. Grant's out. Beth's gone to Maine for the weekend. I sit cool to crash there tonight? Call my service an' have me beeped, okay? Thanks." Click. Receiver to cradle. End of conversation. He sighed and looked around again.

"No one else you can call?" I asked.

"A couple'a friends, but two are way up on West 86th and one's all the way up in fuckin' Washington Heights. Em's the best bet."

"What if she's gone, too?"

"Then I'll crash in Sheep's Meadow in the park, I guess. No big deal. Done it before."

"Are you crazy? You could be mugged or worse doing something like that."

"Done it before," he shrugged.

I scrutinised him, reading his movements, his smile, his words, his eyes – brownish green. They had a life that seemed foreign to most New Yorker's. And, they looked straight into mine. He made a peculiar face, like some myopic man trying to see the next street sign. See into me. He introduced himself as Jeremy Steven Dixon. I introduced myself, tagging that I was native to California. The biggest, shit eating grin lit his face. He was from California, too. A native from Venice. Darkness enveloped us as we talked away an hour, leaning on DO-NUT DELIGHT's brick corner, smoking away my cigarettes and comparing our histories of our time in Los Angeles. We'd done some of the same clubs, some of the same functions at the same time. He was at that warehouse party in Santa Monica where 'X' screeched out songs as crazed revolutionary preppie-meets-punk types pogoed and slam danced into each other for hours. We even had loose associations, mutually known, or barely known people who did the club and underground circuit back then. I finally leaned against the brick wall, amazed by the nightsky.

"You just need a place to crash for the night?" I asked.

"What? You offering?"

"Yeah."

"Well," he started then paused as if a couple hundred thoughts whizzed about in his mind. "You got roommates? Wouldn't they get pissed?"

"No roommates," I said. "You have an axe in that bag?"

"Dirty clothes from the weekend."

"There's a laundromat on my corner."

"I really can crash in the meadow. I wasn't tryin' to wheedle a crash pad."

"You're from home. I got a duty to assist other misguided transplants."

I started walking back toward the neighbourhood. He followed at my heels like an eager pup. "I could . . ." he started, "I could keep tryin' to get Em, maybe, if that's okay."

"I take it this Emma's used to you and your situations?"

"Yeah. She's great. Used to go out, but her brother hates my guts."

"Why?"

"Says I'm a flake. Guess I am at times, but hey, I tell him, I'm from California. You think we should get year 'round snow with all the flakes you say's out there."

"I met a girl here who made me show her my birth certificate to prove to her that I was born there," I said.

"'Cause you're not flaky?"

"'Cause I got brown hair. She thought the Border Patrol was a group that only let blondes into the state."

"Go figure," he said as we stopped by a liquor store to pick up some more butts. He tapped me hesitantly on the shoulder.

"You want a specific brand?" I asked.

"I . . .," he stammered a few more times. "Are you gay?"
"Yeah."
"Just asking," he said. "Your brand's fine by me. Beggars shouldn't be choosers."
"They're all choosy here," I said. "I've had a couple fling the change I gave'em back at me and tell me they only take paper money."
"Then they shouldn't go round asking' if you got any spare change."
"There's no such thing in New York."

*****

We'd sequestered ourselves away in my apartment. Jeremy proved to be an admirable cook, concocting a fresh fruit salad out of the odds and ends and rinds in my refrigerator. Then soup and some scrambled eggs and toast. He had immediately busied himself upon our arrival tidying up my messy place and throwing together a dinner. Nervous energy. The kind that makes people talk and talk and talk. I finally stuck one of the bottles of beer that I kept on hand for guests into his hands and told him to relax. He suddenly became paralysed of body and mute of thought.
"Why're you so nervous?" I said.
"Well . . ." he said. "I . . . I don't know . . . you know. . ."
"If I knew anything at all, I wouldn't be here."
"Here? You got a great apartment."
"Here in New York in the summer," I said.
"I guess . . . If I knew you at all, I guess I wonder if I'd be here at all," he said as he drew a sip from the bottle.
"I haven't showed you my hatchet collection yet, have I?"
He laughed. A loud, nervous release. "Touche Rabbit." He sniffed his arm pits. "I kinda stink, don't I?"
"Not so bad that I have to move downwind."
"Em hates it when I stink even a little bit. Says it's gross."
"You wanna shower? Take a bath? The shower curtain's opaque, so I couldn't secretly stare at you and have masturbatory fantasies," I said.

He smiled slightly as he focused on delicately peeling the label on the bottle. "I guess you just hit the nail on the head," he said. "Guess I got a big fuckin' ego, huh?"

"What," I said. "You thinking I was making you out to be a trick for the night? Well, you're welcome to the floor. You're welcome to my bed, but I am gonna be in it. You wanna sleep, we sleep. You wanna fuck, we can talk. You wanna just be comfortable hanging, we can hang. You wanna have me crush your ego, I will by telling you you're not my type."

"I'll take a shower," he said.

"Got some clothes that might fit you."

"Yours?"

"Most of them," I said. "Some are memories on wire hangers. Men who might have been but weren't."

I had one closet in the tub room. It sort of qualified as a walk-in, if you were skinny enough to slink along between the clothes and boxes and the wall. Only three and a half feet deep, it ran almost the eight foot length of the room. It did have a second doorway, in the kitchen, but that door had been long ago locked, the key lost and thirty or so layers of paint kept it sealed up tight. I turned on the light and slid in, the musty smell of dozens of cedar blocks filtering up my nose. I dug around under the old clear shower curtain I'd hung over the the clothes I rarely wore. The plastic sheet helped keep some of the twenty five billion tons of cosmic dust that daily landed on the Earth off of the cotton and wool garments. I found some madras plaid shirts and a light pair of khakis that I thought would fit him. Remnants of a man who lived with me for a little more than a week. He'd packed up and scooted out while I was at work. These few items he left behind in the hamper. I shimmied out of this hanger coffin, into the tub room. As I looked up, Jeremy was just stepping out of his skivvies. I turned away and hung the shirts on a towel hook as I heard the shower curtain rings skitter and the faucet open wide.

"These shirts should fit you," I said loudly. "They could stand a pressing, though."

His voice rose above the splashy spray of water.

"They're fine! Thanks!"

"I'm going down to the laundromat! I can wash your clothes, if you'd like!?"

He poked his head out between the curtain and the wall. "I'd appreciate it. Thanks."

I mumbled a 'no problem' then gathered up my hamper load into my laundry sack. I stripped the belt from his pants, emptied the pockets and added his wear to my own. Washing supplies tossed in, I scooped up my wallet, keys and change and headed out.

*****

Sploosh-whirring of the washers, thunka-thunking of the dryers, the lazy hum of sluggish flies spiralling up then down, I felt myself being lulled into slumberland. Nobody save myself and some elderly Russians were in this hell pit of a laundromat. I'd read every partially torn up magazine I could find and fantasised that Jeremy had already robbed me blind and boarded a train to Brooklyn. Yet, here I sat, playing some sort of dutiful wife to some absolute stranger. Peter and Paul would call me insane. Even the new fellow, John Wilhelm-Vilhelm might think me a tad scrambled. Well, okay. Maybe it was karmic payback. I picked up three loose pages of a tabloid someone had left behind and reread them.

"Hey!" came the voice. I turned just as Jeremy parked his butt beside me on the bench. He handed me a pint of softening ice cream. "Met yer neighbours. They told me where this place was and that you liked mint chocolate chip." He pulled two plastic spoons from his shirt pocket and handed one to me. I no sooner pried the lid off the ice cream and his spoon was in it, shoveling faster than a dog after a prized bone. Between the two of us, the pint was polished off in a matter of a few minutes. He pitched the empty container and spoons in the trash then we washed up in the grungy sink.

"That was a nice treat," I said.

"Laundry almost done?"

"Done enough. It'll never get completely dry." I grabbed the laundry sack and opened the dryer. He reached in and began to match socks and fold underwear and set them on the nearby counter. "We can do that at the apartment," I said. He just smiled and continued.

"Keep it all as neat as possible," he said. "That's the way I was taught to do it. Besides, this way you can check to make sure you've got all your unmentionables while yer still here."

"My unmentionables or yours," I said.

"Ours," he said. "I used to do my ex-girlfriend's laundry sometimes. Girls' stuff's weird, though. I mean, do you push two bra cups together, ya know, inserting one into the other, or leave'em open an' stack'em like ice cream cones? Sometimes panties are so skimpy there's nothing to fold. Worked in retail for a time. Polyester or silk junk never stayed stacked well. They were always sliding off each other. Then there's the spaghetti strapped top pieces that never would stay on a hanger unless you super-glued it down."

I smoothed out a shirt and folded it meticulously as I watched him all but caress my jockey shorts as he placed them in neat little stacks. Maybe he had a thing for cotton. He held up his own pair of shorts, comparing them with a pair of my briefs. "What?" I asked. "We're the same size. Thirty waist."

"You read my underwear label?"

"Saw it briefly as I tossed it in the washer."

"But . . . are we the same size?"

True. Thirty men could put on the same pair of shorts and there would be thirty different responses. Some fill them out better than others. I cocked an eyebrow and shot him a curious glance. "Is there a need for comparison?"

There was a glint in his eyes. A very slight smile bordering on nervous fear. The glint faded quickly as he turned back to the duties at hand. "I'm sorry . . ."

"About what?" I asked.

"That was a loaded question. Sometimes my mouth runs off before I think."

"Subtle but teasing propositions?"

"I didn't mean it to be one."

"Okay," I said.

"I had a guy like me once, ya know," he said as he slid garments into the sack. "Actually he was one of my best friends. He told me he was gay, an' I shrugged and said, 'so what,' thinking that it didn't matter. And it didn't. To me. But then, I kinda teased him some. Big mistake."

"Why?"

"He misunderstood. Thought I was interested in him. He was in love with me. I went over his place one night and he . . . he like had this whole scene laid out in his head how the night was gonna happen."

"He tried to seduce you?"

"Kind of. I screwed up 'cause I knew early on where the dinner, the conversation, the whole thing was going . . . I should have stopped it early on. Could have. All it would've taken was for me to steer the course away from his plan, but I didn't. I played along."

"How far?"

"To the point where he kissed me. I freaked." I picked up the laundry sack and we headed out of the dank, humid hell hole onto the hellish street. As we walked, I let Jeremy relay his story. "I just pushed him aside and bolted from his apartment. Haven't talked to him or even seen him since."

"Why'd you let it go so far?"

"I liked the idea of him being attracted to me. Fucked it up. Big time."

"I've been on his end before. Only with me it went a lot farther. He's dead now."

"AIDS?"

"A pile up on the 405 freeway in Los Angeles."

"How much farther did it go with you?"

"We . . . bonded. A few times."

"You loved him."

"Very much," I said. Memories of him flashed about in my head. My January slide show that had welcomed in each successive new year with notions of how things might have been, how we might have ended up. It was easy to lose myself to fantasy, to waste away hours in bed straining to remember his smell, the feel of his skin, the taste of his mouth, his cum, his sweat . . . Sweat. It still trickled down from my brow, though nighttime cloaked us like a fichu. Humidity is never ending.

Jeremy had fallen silent, staring blankly at the sidewalk that treadmilled by under our feet as we walked up the stoop and into the building. I suddenly felt tired of being tired as we lumbered up the steps and entered my apartment. In the darkness, I could see the blinking red light on my answering machine. I hit the playback button as I dumped the clothes on the bed. Jeremy picked out his belongings as the message from his friend, Emma, played. She was back and wanted him to come over. Simple and direct. Very much to the point. I handed him the phone. He dialled. I took some clothes to the closet and stuffed them in, trying not to listen, but hearing his conversation with this mysterious Emma. More details came out about his apartment that he hadn't told me. He was four months behind in rent for his illegal sublet, as he evidently had been once before. The lessor was confiscating his belongings until he came up with the money. Then there was a whisper about connecting to some coke. I was sure he wasn't referring to a refreshing soft drink. Now my mind whirled about a bit, cognisant of the fact that even good people get in over their heads and often resort to illegal means to rectify their problems, yet I kept flashing on images of duplicitous characters from all sorts of movies and novels, out to scam, out to flim-flam any and all. Still, he'd probably well noticed that I didn't have the proverbial pot to piss in, let alone anything of merit to steal. It wasn't my business. Some years ago, after Rex had been killed in a tangle of fenders and grill work on the freeway, after my friend Lisa and her uncle, Carl, had put me on a path to sober living, after sex became a plague ridden event, after all semblance of emotions had been walled up neatly into a dark corner inside me, after everything formerly internalised had been usurped by detached observation and analysis, I found the best defense was to remain as best as possible an observer, a possible arbitrator, separate in all events and situations. This was supposed to be a part of the difference between being an adult and a child. The child reacts to his needs, most often not knowing how to effect a change for himself and seeks assistance from others to help him along. The adult must be able to facilitate a child, any child, even the child locked within himself. In doing so, however, the adult tends to lose that spirit inside of wonderment and an openness to all possibilities – possibilities once offered by a shiny, strong and stout-hearted dragon. It was like being in the dark, again. Not like being a predator waiting to strike, to act out of fear-based needs. No. This dark was a cloak. To bury myself under and feel safe. Safe from the outside. Safe from myself. Now, hearing Jeremy's conversation I wondered if I'd made another error in judgement. I didn't care, or want to care, how he survived in this city, just so long as he survived. All people lie, even to their closest of friends. I wasn't surprised that he'd lied to me about his whole mess. Still, it bothered me and I didn't like that it bothered me. This meant that somehow, he'd stuck a finger through my wall and pulled down my blanket of blind security a fraction. Thinking of feeling emotion and actually feeling it are two very different things. Something I didn't like.

I came back into the room just as he was hanging up the phone. He looked a bit defeated, very weary yet perturbed. I toyed with picking up a few items and placing them back in other places they really didn't belong. Waiting. It was his call. He made it.

"She's home."

"Okay," I said.

"I should go over there."

"Do what you gotta do." He didn't move. At all. Just stared at the floor. I picked up his gym bag and placed his clean garments inside. He looked up at me, watched me zip his bag shut and leave it on the floor beside him.

"I appreciate what you've done."

"I know."

He rose from his seat and gave me a rather sudden hug and peck on the lips. His abruptness flushed his cheeks red. I smiled, handed him his bag and escorted him to the door. He paused briefly in the hallway, pulling a scrap of paper from his wallet and handing it to me.

"That's my service number. The one bill I always make sure is paid."

I took the number and pocketed it, adding, "I'm in the book. If you can find a phone book in Manhattan that hasn't been shredded to bits."

"Thanks," he whispered, then turned and descended the stairs. I stood in the doorway, listening. His footsteps faded until I finally heard the squeaky front door clack shut. I was just about to seal myself back into my cocoon when Paul poked his head out of his apartment.

"Well, well, well . . ." he said with that somewhat obnoxious 'I get it' look on his face.

"Well nothing," I said.

"Quite attractive."

"Quite."

He stepped out into the hallway, revealing Peter also listening at the door. "So give."

"His name's Jeremy. He's from California. I met him on the street. We visited for a time, now he's gone over to his girlfriend's house."

Peter and Paul looked at each other with a smirk, quietly muttering 'gender bender' in unison.

I leaned against my doorjamb, cocking a brow at them. "We didn't bend anything. I doubt I'll hear from him, save maybe once, again."

Peter furrowed his brow, studying me. He whispered to Paul, "I think he's telling the truth."

"But didn't he buy you ice cream?" Paul asked.

"Yeah. For doing his laundry."

"Did you get his number at least?" said Paul.

"His service number. I told him I'm in the book. Let him call me, if he has a mind to."

"Ohhh . . ." said Paul.

"He's playing the game," said Peter.

"There's no game," I said. "He's a nice guy with some problems I don't want to get involved with unless there's a reason for me to get involved. Got it?"

"Okay," said Paul. "There's no reason to get snitty."

"We were just thinking it'd be good for you to have a boyfriend," said Peter.

"Well, this isn't him. You two have a good night."

They nodded their departure and slunk back into their apartment as I parked myself in mine. I couldn't help but toy with the notion they'd had, of me 'dating' Jeremy. Still, it was stupid for me to fantasise after only a few hours with the man. I stretched back out on my bed, letting the sticky cooling air try to ebb in through opened windows. I felt like a holiday turkey parked on rack in an open oven. Stewing but not basting in my own juices. It's difficult to fall asleep some summer nights. Difficult, but not impossible.

*****

The beach on a January day. Overcast. Soothing, lapping waves caressed the dune flanked shore. Gulls swooped down, tagging the water, dredging up specks of food and I walked alone, isolated on a narrow band of land. There's traffic on the ocean. Boats. Heading north, heading south. I heard my name being called. Distant. Echoing. Fog horns blast, drowning the voices. I can't see them. Obscured forms, blurring like watercolours. Up in the air. Another streak. Crimson bleeding green. The fog swelled up and rolled in toward shore. Obliteration.

The telephone jarred me awake. I'd forgotten to reset my answering machine. Rubbery legs ambled toward the five alarm blast. "Hello?" I said. It was him. Jeremy. Had I already been asleep two hours? I had. He and Emma had a fight. Could he come back? Spend the night? I agreed. Too quickly I thought as I hung up the phone. Christ why wasn't life simple? It was simple. For a time. This was why I had resolved not to become involved in people's lives again. It all took up too much energy. There was too much uncertainty. Still, I was the one who'd made the initial offer. I had to live with my action and its consequence. At least for the night.

*****

I sat awake and waited. One hour passed into two, into three . . . Somewhere down the line, my eyes gave in to fatigue and I drifted off into a dead calm sleep. This too shall pass certainly applied. I hadn't been asleep for more than half an hour when the phone jarred me awake again. I was ready to curse a blue haze over him for being so rude when I was cut off by a very, very distraught woman on the other end of the line. She wanted desperately to speak with Jeremy. I told her that I had a few choice words to say to him as well, once he showed up. That set her off, spinning into a panic. It was Emma. Evidently Jeremy had left her place hours ago. She calmed down enough to explain what had happened. An argument. Very base in nature. Mostly about her brother whom Jeremy admitted disliked him. She wanted me to meet her, to go out on the streets in the middle of the night and look for him. I tried to politely beg off, but to no avail. Tears and soft pleading forced me to pull on my shoes, run a comb through my hair and journey out into no man's land to hunt down this vagabond.

*****

We met at Sheridan Square. Two strangers standing alone on a corner looking out cautiously to any passing face in the dark. She was an attractive woman, approximately my own age with long dark brown hair. Pale, pale skin. Bright gray eyes. Petite. And cold. She shivered as we quickly introduced ourselves to each other then inquired about Jeremy.

She told me that he had a problem with cocaine. That he used to use it, sell it over around Second Avenue and Thirteenth Street. However, somewhere along the way his abuse ate up his profits.

"Being ousted from his place's got him wigged out some," she said.

"What? You think we should try hunting for him in his old territory?"

"He knew some skank over on Fourteenth who'd get him high so she could screw him."

It was late. I was tired. I didn't want to go hunting a mile down the road for someone who so obviously wanted to be lost at that moment. Emma's eyes teared a bit as she stared in all directions. "You know the address?" I said.

*****

The cab dumped us off in front of an old brownstone. No one seemed to be lurking about, but I still didn't feel comfortable as we climbed the steps. The front door was made of safety glass. The upper section a web of fractures fanning out from a shattered indentation. Someone's fist or head had tried to plow through, but the wire netting in the glass had held fast. Emma pushed on the door. It gave easily. So much for security.

The stairs, the balustrade, the walls all looked like they'd been chewed on by millions of mice. Twenty-five watt bulbs softened the harshness of it all. We climbed two flights, the stairs creaking with every step. Down the hall. Apartment 3G. Emma listened at the door. Heavy metal, barely audible, leaked out. Then I heard it. A distinctly male groan of pleasure. Emma heard it, too. Her eyes hardened as she twisted the doorknob and threw the door wide open. The sight was something to behold. Jeremy lay nude, sprawled across a large bed in the darkened room, the young woman who lived there was buck naked with her pelvis straddled over his face, polishing her privates with his tongue. They were lost in their own coked-out reverie. Blind to the moment, I only saw his slickened face and matted hair and his jutting erection. My own crotch stirred at this hedonistic vision. Before I knew it Emma was on them both, knocking the girl off of him and slapping Jeremy hard. Neither seemed to know what had hit them, their eyes mere slits straining to see, their tongues thickened by intoxicants, stifling their speech. She tried to force Jeremy up.

"Help me!" I jumped to. "Find his clothes and get him

dressed!" she said.

The clothes were easily identified. I grabbed them up in a ball, set them on the edge of the bed, then grabbed Jeremy's arms, yanked him up, then picked him up like the proverbial sack of potatoes and hoisted his limp body up onto my shoulder. Emma slammed the clothes into my gut and I carried him out into the hallway. All I heard was the door slam, then Emma's screeching and slapping going on. Jeremy's rigid cock stabbed my shoulder. His ass brushed my cheek. I dropped the clothes, and, as I strained to up right him against the wall, I admittedly allowed my fingers to quickly trace over his rear. This wasn't the time, though, for my own desires to flair. I braced him up, grabbed his shorts and tried to talk him through the act of stepping into them. As I guided his feet through the openings, his hands came down to rest on my shoulders to steady himself. The head of his dick bobbed against my nose, a tacky drop of pre-cum gluing us together for a nanosecond. I quickly pulled the shorts up as I rose out of temptation's way and pressed him back against the wall.

"Fucked up?" he groaned.

"You sure did. Come on."

I got his shirt on him, missing a few button holes in the process. I let him finish the task himself. This all only took a matter of a minute or two. Emma charged out, slamming the door behind her, barking at us to follow as she flew down the stairs. I stuffed his socks into my back pocket and rooted him in his shoes.

Out on the street, Emma was seething. She said nothing but led the way to Second Avenue where she managed to hail a gypsy cab. She jumped in. I helped Jeremy in, then slid in beside him. Before the cabby could ask,Emma looked blankly at me, "Where do you live?"

"I thought you wanted to take him . . ."

She cut me off. "Not tonight. Not looking and smelling like he's been with that four dollar whore."

"Emma . . ." he started.

"Shut up, Jeremy."

I told the cabby my address. As we drove, Emma said

nothing. She just stared out her window at the passing neighbourhoods. Jeremy leaned into me, his head slumped on my shoulder. I could smell her. On his face, in his head. As if he'd managed to slide his head all the way into her. His crotch was still straining. Tenting the material with unresolved lust. We sat in silence the rest of the ride.

When we reached my building, Emma said she'd call me the next afternoon sometime and thanked me for shepherding him back. I pulled a very groggy and rubber-kneed Jeremy from the cab and slowly guided him up the stoop.

It took forever to help him up the stairs to my apartment. Once inside, he collapsed on the bed. I set about undressing him, hoping to get him into the shower to rinse away this stale scent of sex. Once stripped down to his shorts, I stepped away from him to study his form. I'd only gotten a glimpse before when he showered earlier. A very, very appealing body lay splayed out before me. A large wet spot on his underwear indicated that he'd already climaxed. I once again grabbed him by his arms to pull him up to his feet, only this time, he became animated. His hands grasped my head and shoved my face into his crotch.

"Suck it . . ." he groaned. Moist with sweat, with dribbles of piss, with cum, my nostrils inhaled the smell of him. My face felt the lumps of his cock, his balls, knead against me. I pushed myself up, off of him. I grabbed his shorts and yanked them off. A thick glob of white cum covered his pubic hair. He was uncircumcised. I'd failed to notice that before. Concupiscence stirred. He was beautiful. Still, it wasn't the right time to entertain this notion. Had this happened some years back, when rational thought was very often blighted, I wouldn't have hesitated to suckle on him, to feel the fold of flesh loll about in my mouth, coaxing the head of his member out to play. That was then. Now, now I yanked him to his feet, slapping his face gently to revive him a bit.

"You have to shower," I said.

For the first time, his eyes seemed to open, almost

completely. He was sad. Perhaps embarrassed. Perhaps feeling a bit guilty. I helped him to the tub room and into the shower. His legs were weak from exhaustion. I stripped down and climbed into the tub with him. I helped him wash away the event of the night, scrubbing his face, his hair, his body, making him wash thoroughly his penis and his ass. No tell tale signs, no hint of sexual scent. Squeaky clean from ears to toes. I kept the water hot, keeping my own cock from rising in anticipation, but making the apartment once again humid. I helped him towel dry. By now he was awakening. I had thought cocaine to bean upper. I hadn't been a coke hound in my days of abuse. I'd found it a useless drug as it clogged my sinuses and gave me a headache. I had preferred liquor and speed. Real speed in pill or capsule form – hearts, crosses, black beauties and the like. When I got him into bed, I crawled in beside him and turned out the light. It was so very, very late that it was early. The voice rose in the darkness.

"I fucked up."

"It's over. Get some sleep."

"I'm sorry," he said. I could sense that he was crying. Quiet, unobtrusive tears. I rolled into him closing the distance.

"What are you afraid of?"

"Everything." My hand caressed his head. He instantly drew into me and let loose with great heaves of sobbing. I didn't know what to say, if I should say anything at all. I kept my mouth shut and wrapped my arms about him and let him cry himself to sleep.

*****

In the haze of the morning, I could feel my arm, numbed beyond life, crushed beneath the weight of his body. I pushed him a bit, hoping he'd briefly stir and roll over. He was as dead and unanimated as a storyboard corpse. With some persistence, I was able to free myself, though I had to spend the next ten minutes slapping and massaging my arm to awaken the circulation. I immediately grabbed some fresh skivvies and crawled to the shower to revitalise. Somewhere between the cream rinse cycle and the shave I heard him gently padding about out in the kitchen. The noise subsided. As I finished my ritual, I was sure he was either making us breakfast or he'd skipped out completely. I opted to wait until I was through to find out.

The moist steam hung in the air as I stood before the sink trying to blow dry my hair. Trickles of sweat cascaded from my hair line. A pointless venture. For a brief instant, I thought I could see through the wall, like Superman, seeing what Mr. Vilhelm-Wilhelm was up to. I'd have to eventually introduce myself, as these paper thin walls breed familiarity, especially in the toilet where he could hear every bit of business I was up to. I stowed away the useless dryer, slipped on my shorts and hung up the towel. I yanked a fresh t-shirt from the closet and slid into it before checking up on my charge.

He was before the window, his left arm up-stretched, bracing himself against the casement. A glass of water, dripping slightly, poised in his right hand. Beautiful, nude form and cowlicked hair made silhouette by early morning sun forcing its way in dredged up memories in me. Flickers of visions of the past, of being painfully in love. This was a sight I longed to see on Sunday mornings after an expressive, intense night of satiating lust and desires. He took another sip of water, set the glass on the sill and continued to stare out into the void.

"Sometimes I just wanna be a mussel stuck to some rock under the sea. Rooted. A hard shell protecting me," he said.

"Eventually someone would come along and rip you from your rock," I said as I stepped into my walking shorts.

"I'd let them catch me in a month with an R in it," he said. "Seems I'm toxic anyhow." He turned toward me, hands behind him, leaning against the wall. "I was gonna hurry and get dressed, but I figured you'd already seen me in the buff, so what's the point?"

"Feeling vulnerable?"

"And guilty and embarrassed. Why'd you'n she have to come looking for me?"

"Wasn't my idea," I said. "But, she seemed desperate to find you. Why'd you run off?"

"Her brother makes me feel like such a fucking loser. I just . . . Fuck, I don't know. No place I felt I could go, maybe. Sheila likes me."

"But, do you like her?" I said as I dug through cassettes. I found a tape, stuck it in and fast-forwarded toward the end.

"Not really . . ." I turned the volume very, very low, cuing up a song. When I heard the tail notes of one song, I stopped it. I went to Jeremy, slipped my arms about him slowly and locked him into a hug. He hesitated for a moment, then pressed himself against me and held on tight. "I'm sorry," he whispered.

I broke our stance, turned to the bed, pulled back the covers and told him to lie down. Again, he hesitated. I told him I thought he should sleep some more. He nestled into the bed. I drew the top sheet up about him, then grabbed keys, wallet, socks and shoes. I said I would be back in awhile.Then, as I headed out the door, I turned up the volume a bit on the cassette player and turned it on. Blondie's soothing lullaby, "Sound-A-Sleep," began.

*****

Peter and Paul weren't home. For them, this was unusual. They rarely had money to splurge on something as simple as breakfast. Then again, maybe they'd managed to find some way to get out to the beach.

As I bounded out the foyer, I ran into the boys with a rather handsome looking fellow. They introduced me to my new neighbour. It was John Wilhelm. Aryan stock indeed. Tall, dirty blonde, bright, bright blue eyes. A very angular but strong face and jaw. A sturdy sort of peasant stock he was all right, but nonetheless very attractive. He'd invited them to breakfast and wasn't it a shame that I hadn't heard them rapping on my door. They'd knocked rather gently, as they had heard me stumble in with Jeremy late and thought I'd gotten lucky. I quickly gave them the drab details of an unconsummated night. They seemed more disappointed for me than I could have ever been for myself.

"So you left the sleeping prince up in your bed?" said Paul. "You should be there, comforting him some more. He's gotta bend a bit after all that's been said and done."

"You're missing the point," I said.

Peter pulled Paul along. "He does that all the time. We're going up for a cat nap."

They said their thanks and good-byes to John, leaving us alone on the stoop. He smiled at me and shrugged. "Interesting fellows," he said. "Where were you headed to?"

"No place particular," I said. "I've already pissed away most of this weekend, so I thought I'd just walk aimlessly around until some notion of what to do with my life strikes me into another reality."

"You want some company? I don't really feel like being cooped up all day. Besides, the paint fumes are still airing out."

"Sure."

"You mind waiting a minute or two? I just wanna get something, brush my teeth, use the can . . ." he said.

"Go . . ." I said. He hustled inside, his great massive weight seemingly breaking through every step of the stairs as he bounded up. The way they echoed, I thought the old building was finally going to topple down around me. I fished the pack of cigarettes and lighter from my pockets.The pack had gotten scrunched a bit since the previous night. I straightened out a butt and lit it. It was going to be another hazy, lazy day. The sun climbed steadily toward infinity, sending its searing rays down to reflect back off of glass and concrete to bake us all to a well done crispness.

I sat there, staring at the people milling about, most of them probably only out to avoid their already warming ovens called apartments. It was a bit much to fathom, that so many people could live so cloistered together in one neighbourhood, let alone one city. Neighbourhoods themselves become almost like small towns wherein everyone knew who was supposed to be there and suspicious of any unclaimed persons loitering about. Here we all were, bottled up in some cosmic microwave oven, waiting to see who's guts exploded first. This was far cry from the notions carried forth from childhood that the world was a place holding promise, dangling the wonders and excitement of a future for one to chase after. But that future tarnished and fell by the wayside like a dragon I once knew. Spat upon by an endless series of crappy jobs, a shrinking market place, and mounting debts. The future proved to be expensive. Many of us got caught up in chasing the promise, unaware of the roadblocks being fabricated. Education was the highest goal. So . . . So what that the universities were burgeoning with students. So what that nobody told you in your Junior year of high school the one of the criteria for entry was to have maintained a minimum of a 3.9 grade point average. So what that the universities were so inundated with applicants that they could choose two thousand of the world's best candidates. Those with straight A averages, with resumés filled with school activities and charitable works. So what that seven-eighth's of those applicants never had to work a day in their lives as their parents sacrificed and spent thousands upon thousands of dollars over the years to keep their progeny one step ahead of the game. Those parents who were in control of the lives and livelihoods of the parents of the rest of us. In those days, the rich got Baked Alaska. The plebeians got tapioca pudding. The rich ate filet mignon and asparagus. The plebs ate Hamburger Helper and canned corn. The CEO's pulled in more income by cutting their employees' wages, by breaking up unions. The leaders sold out to other rising nations, careful to make sure that duplicitous cheques were cashed and secure in the bank or invested in solid stocks. The worker ants were left to longer hours, lower wages, unemployment lines, higher rents and mortgage payments. Whoopee for the American way. Even worker children who maintained the old standards of getting a 'solid' college preparatory education, who had to forego many resume lifting school activities in order to work twenty to forty hours a week to save their minimum wage earnings to help foot their college tuition bills, who got good to very good scores on their S.A.T. exams, were considered substandard to these American institutions of higher learning in the late 1970s and early 1980s. I'd actually seen Departmental scholarships be given to students' whose parents combined incomes exceeded one hundred thousand dollars or more, while many bright and talented worker children were told to go beg, borrow or steal what they needed, provided these levels of higher learning deigned to allow them entry into a Freshman class.

Hello. Welcome to Blah-Blah University. You're middle-class. We really didn't want you. Your parents aren't rich enough, nor poor enough. However, we had to take some of you. I mean, how would it look otherwise? Tuition will be ten thousand dollars, payable up front. Lab fees will be another fifteen hundred bucks, payable up front. We're generously giving you a scholarship. One thousand dollars! Be thankful. Go to the Financial Aid office and fill out fifty or so forms you'll need to apply for loans. There's the GSL, the NDSL, the FISL, Perkins Loans, and . . . just all sorts of government agencies you can beg for your tuition fees. Of course you'll have to do quite a song and dance routine for them to be eligible. Then once your loans have been approved, we all can run you ragged and stress you out so wonderfully well just trying to get that cheque, you'll need to see one of our doctors at Student Health Services about that pre-ulcerous condition your stomach will be in. Fees for Student Health Services are not included in the quoted price. That's an additional four hundred dollars. Now, just walk right over to the Student Housing Office to attempt to secure a residence and you'll be treated like one of your very own dirt poor and diseased relations that you want to have nothing to do with. Good day. Enjoy your years at Blah-Blah University. Next!

Now here we all merged, in these mega-cities of urban decay, hunting for careers, which require more and more specialisation as the years move on. The answer to that? Get more education. If you can't afford it because your credit's over extended and you owe everyone and God twenty-five thousand dollars or more, don't fret. Get another low paying McJob. Your great-grandparents had to work sixteen hour days. Did you hear them complaining? Got a five hundred square foot shoe box that you live in? Pack yourself and five of your closest friends into one to split the rent and utilities. Working sixteen hour days for dick-squat wages, you won't have the time or energy to squawk and argue about petty little things like who's turn it is to clean the toilet. You won't care. Need a car? Car insurance? Funds to pay for the insurance, gas and maintenance? Simple. Move to a city with a respectable public transportation system. Already live in one? Then the city must be compact enough to enable you to walk almost everywhere you need to go. Wearing out your shoes walking everywhere? Go to thrift stores and buy cheap beat up old sneakers for just two hours wages. Cook at home. Plain pasta, rice, beans, day old bread, spoiling vegetables on sale. You can eat cheap. Do this for the next ten years of your life and you'll be free from debt. Your expensive education will be paid off and then some. You'll be too old to vie for a new career. Besides there won't be any jobs left worth moving up in. If you're lucky enough not to get laid off to make room for a younger and cheaper employee who won't squawk about benefits being cut because they'll have never had a job with benefits, you'll die peacefully from a massive coronary right at your cramped little cube in your cramped office in your high rise with Sick Building Syndrome. Dead before you're forty years old. What more could you want? It's the American way. In the meanwhile, make the best of your life, caged in this cityscape. There are those worse off than you.

I sat and stared at these worker ants milling about. Wreckage from a shipwreck called the U.S.S. American Dream. I could only hope those closing up our ranks had figured out this disaster before they continued on.

There was a tap on my shoulder. John Wilhelm stood

beside me, a bulging backpack hung loosely about his shoulder. I snubbed out my cigarette and poked his gear. "You a survivalist or something?"

"Call it my security blanket," he said. We trudged happily on.

*****

He had me positioned in Alice's lap. Alice being the great Alice in Wonderland sculpture in Central Park. The winsome waif was three times my size, but almost as cute as the Disney version of the character. John's camera whirred away. I felt ridiculous. I hated having my picture taken. It seemed so touristy. He continued to click away as I climbed down from the giant's lap and parked myself on a mushroom step.

"No more," I said.

"I got another roll."

"Take pictures of tourists or buildings then."

"You're more interesting," he said as he continued to click a way.

"I look like a horse."

"Horses are handsome."

We hadn't said much as we trekked by foot, then bus, up to the park. He was a spacial artist. Translated, that means that space is a viable art form, to be shaped and created. I'd always just considered those who 'created' space to be designers. Wrong again. Always wrong. My special talent. Most of our babble was about this concept. Once we arrived at the sculpture, he whipped out this camera as I climbed up into Alice's lap, hoping to reclaim some lost essence of childhood. In an instant, between his snapping away, or whirring or whatever sound that camera made, I had a flash. An alarming insight. Maybe I'd had it before. I couldn't tell. In that moment, the realisation was fresh. I'd never really been a child. I mean, I had physically been a kid, at some point in time, but I'd never felt like a kid even when I was one. I was one of those many children born old – mildly, chronically worried about anything and everything, preferring adult company to kids, always projecting to see myself as I was now, an adult. I knew fantasy but never lost sight of its perspective as just that, a fantasy. Now, here I was trying to reclaim something I'd never really owned. Innocence. I was having sexual thoughts at the age of six, though they weren't X-rated thoughts. Sexual's too harsh a term. Sensual thoughts. Nudity. I was intrigued by nudity. Male and female forms. Their peculiarities, their beauty, their ugliness. Anyhow, I knew I never believed those games we played. Never believed that I was really Captain Kirk or Mr. Spock. Never believed that I was really that flying monkey on *Space Ghost*, a fanciful cartoon we used to watch. Still I tried damned hard to be a kid and to believe. I endured my brother and his friend shoving me off the back porch roof, telling me to fly, then dropping twelve feet to land splat in the middle of Mrs. B's flowers. Maybe because I didn't believe I could fly, I never did.Mumps were reality. Begging to play Little League baseball to make my father proud, then fearing and loathing it once I was committed to a team was a reality. Never honestly believing girls had cooties was a reality. Fear was a reality. Suspicion was a reality. Was the woman who lived in the old Victorian house on Palm Street really a witch who snatched kids from the street, fried their whole bodies in lard, then hung the corpses in her windows at night a reality? No. Was the suspicion of this woman's character though warranted? Possibly. Maybe the reality was that she had a healthy suspicion of children. Maybe she had this suspicion because other kids had tormented and teased her unmercifully as a child. That legendary witch house did exist on Palm Street. The suspicion and my fear drew me to that house one day. I flew solo at seven. I crossed Lincoln Street one day on my way home from school and walked right up to the house and just stared at it. I wanted to see what the other kids had seen. Wanted to see if the ghost of my fried corpse hung in one of the windows. My heart pounded as I stared it down for what seemed to be hours. It was only minutes, though. A hostile inquiry shouted by a nosey neighbour stirred my feet and they moved. I raced half the way home.

So here I was, decades later, sitting on a sculpted metal mushroom, in Central Park, with another man I'd just met who was hell bent on taking my picture. Click. Whirrrr . . . Click.He wouldn't stop. I hopped up and started walking away.

"Okay, okay," he said.

"Thank you," I said as he stowed away his toy. "I don't like having my picture taken. Someone might use it for voodoo."

"Don't be so negative."

"Cautious." Suspicious.

"You've been in New York too long."

"The magic's gone. What can I say?"

We walked along, out of the park. John Wilhelm fell into silence and peered about lazily, drinking in all the sights. He seemed nice. Then again, Jeremy seemed nice. My mind worked overtime, trying to quickly assess and analyse the quiet giant beside me. I felt like Mutt and Jeff. I seemed to attract strangers, transient people, all the time. In a way, there felt to be some security in knowing that they'd be gone within a limited amount of time.

"You hungry yet?" he asked.

"A bit."

"Let me buy you lunch."

"Normally, I like to carry my own weight, but since I'm broke I'll let you."

*****

It was a diner, like any other diner in the city. Worn, brown vinyl booth seats, sticky formica topped tables, never any packets of sweetener in the caddies, but always a shaker of salt and a large container of sugar three quarters full. I'd found New Yorkers, for the most part, to be opposed to black coffee. If you ordered a regular coffee to go, they gave you a syrupy concoction, one-third coffee, one-third milk and one-third sugar. Fine for a child, but not for me. Anyhow, while I was hungry, the muggy weather quelled my taste for things heavy, fatty or fried. I had a boring bowl of sliced bananas, half a grapefruit and toast. John Wilhelm, however, had that full, heart-stopping, fried up, bacon, egg and coffee breakfast. It looked good, but I knew if I ate likewise, my stomach would be doing back flips the rest of the day.

As we ate we talked further, delving into more private areas of our lives. He was only two years older than me, yet had been married and divorced before he was twenty-two. He'd been born into a rather wealthy family in Delaware, and was expected, upon completion of college, to follow into his family's business of property development. When his young wife learned from him that he had other ambitions – eclectic ambitions – she chose to escape the marriage, obtain a healthy settlement and move on to find a husband who'd be able to provide her with the security she desired. He held no malice toward her for her decision. He said he understood fear, therefore understood that her actions were driven by fear. They'd remained on friendly terms with each other until she found the man she was looking for and remarried. Now, here he was just a couple of years later, living in this city, developing his craft as an artist. I also learned that he was able to sustain this lifestyle through a nominal trust fund his grandmother had long ago established for him. I was often envious of those with financial freedom like his, as it allowed for pursuit of broader interests. I wasn't so fortunate. Few of my friends were, either. I briefly expounded on my alcoholic past, problems encountered, when and why I'd moved to the city, blah, blah, blah. He'd inquired about my charge, Jeremy. I explained, succinctly, some, not all, of what had transpired, ending it with the morning's encounter.

"Why'd you take him in?" he asked.

"Why not?"

"Most people have a healthy suspicion of others, especially in New York."

"Actually, I've found people here, while at times on the loud and hostile side, to be basically friendly. The ones I find cold and detached are the newly arrived or the overly victimised," I said.

"And you're neither."

"Maybe."

"Good enough. Always walk the fence," he said as he shovelled the final forkful into his mouth. He was easy to be around. While he was attractive, I wasn't attracted to him. He was most like a large, clunky golden retriever. I wanted to press him a bit more on his ex-wife, but his brief remarks indicated a reticence to expound any further than on what he had already given.

He paid the check and we ambled out. The day was pissing away. I didn't care. Monday would roll around in no time and blend into every other Monday past, present and future. Time itself was a mobius strip. A never ending loop we all stumble onto and tread hastily or lazily from birth to death. In death the treadmill stops, but only for a time.

*****

Jeremy was out on the stoop, sunning with Peter and Paul. They were laughing, mildly clowning around. For some reason, Jeremy's jocularity annoyed me a bit. Did he turn himself off and on with the ease of new faucet? He tossed me a cursory greeting with a nod of his head, then Paul grabbed his attention with another cynical commentary. Laughter. John said he was going on up to see how many cockroaches had died from the paint fumes. He invited me up. Jeremy's ears perked up and offered me a piece of the stoop beside him. I told John I'd be up in a minute, but I didn't take Jeremy up on his offer to sit next to him. I guess I glared at him a moment too long for he hung his head in a guilty fashion and tugged at the hairs on his leg.

Peter noticed the slight, silent admonishment. He nudged Paul and suggested they go up and grab some sodas. Paul, being the inquisitive, nay, nosey, creature he was, argued the point of the two of them trekking upstairs to grab some cans. Why not just toss them in a plastic grocery sack if you couldn't carry them? Peter must've shot him some secret look for Paul finally 'got it'. They offered for Jeremy to come on up with them for a while when he felt inclined to. Jeremy nodded. They went in. I finally took a set near but not next to him.

"Glad to see you're having a good time," I said.

"If you can't be fair, bite it," he said.

"Okay, I can't be fair. How about being honest?"

"They're funny. They made me laugh. Is that so wrong?"

No it wasn't. I felt small. Not that small, but small enough. "You're right."

A slight glimmer of a smile crept back onto his lips."I guess it sorta seemed like I didn't care, huh."

"Honestly? I'll be honest. My big fucking word. I was jealous."

"Of what?"

"You're fucking incredible looking. At least I think so. You're personable. Except for being a bit fucked up, you're really pretty nice."

He laughed. "I modelled. Still do when I can pull it together. I hate it."

"You make money?"

"Made it. Spent it. Most of it going up my nose," he said. "My agent still gets me gigs occasionally. My type's still popular in Japan." A beat. "You really think I'm good looking?"

"Yeah."

He seemed both amused and aghast at the concept, snickering a bit. "You're nice looking."

"Compliments don't need to be returned. I'm okay. No door prize to salivate over, though. Okay's good enough. Very attractive people and very ugly people stand out in a crowd. Me, I look like everyone's distant cousin on their mother's side of the family."

"That can be special," he said as he cocked his head and tried to lock my gaze.

"I know the concept," I said. "Familiarity. Comfortability. Like an ear of corn."

"A Christmas tree."

"A jack-o-lantern."

"I love Halloween," he said. "License to express yourself without judgement."

"Go on up and play with the boys. But, remember to give Emma a call, please. She deserves it." He nodded in agreement and headed in. I waited a moment, letting him get ahead of me,then I went upstairs to John's apartment.

*****

We sipped cranberry juice, diluted by melting ice, while seated in some bizarre, cube shaped, down filled chairs. This, I was sure, was as close as I would ever come to being parked on a cloud. Though my chair all but swallowed me whole, John's lumbering form still managed to spill out all over. The chairs fit the apartment. It was . . . incongruous . . . perhaps. Eclectic. Weird. David Hockney meets Disney meets the Jetsons meets the Antique Guild. Everything sprayed everywhere like a tomcat's urine. Everything had its history. Its reason for being. The plaster-of-paris miniature Miss Liberty. The fifty year old anniversary clock. The boomerang formica and Hepplewhite table. Native American and Persian rugs. A thirty plus year-old ashtray from Woolworth's. The weathered, grayed picket gate that hung on one wall was a treat. He called it his escape route. On the other side of it was the real him. The responsible him, sans trust fund dollars, beginning a white collar career, still with the wife and planning for little Eric and Erica Wilhelm's future college funding. Service and enslavement lay in wait just beyond that gate.

"What if it's not that," I asked.

"Good," he said with a smile. "You understand the game."

"Games aren't important in the all-around," I said.

"Tell that to children. Tell that to sports fans. Tell that to the housewives in the Bingo parlour."

"They foster competition. They foster envy. They foster hatred."

"They build courage. They build appreciation. They bring joy," he countered.

"Sorry, but I find your choices still to be fear based," I said.

"Where's the fear in joy?"

"We're talking about the joy found in games. People are usually only joyful if they or their team has thoroughly trashed the opponent. They revel in the defeat of others. Joy shouldn't be born out of someone else's misery, should it?" I said.

"Do you always look for the negative?"

"There's always the duality," I said as I set my empty glass on the coffee table. "That's how I've come to view everything."

"Don't you find that your view generates a reaction that has consequence on your choice of action?"

I only had to think for a moment. "Yes. It does." I wanted a cigarette. I felt a debate coming on and I wasn't comfortable in any debate without the reassurance of a cancer stick to accentuate my thoughtful pauses.

John grabbed my glass and headed into the kitchen. "Think about what you'd see behind that gate."

I stared at the gate. I thought about a nicotine blast. My clothes felt tacky from off and on sweating. Was my deodorant failing me? How much oil, grime and bacteria was there caked on my skin? My hair surely looked greasy and clumpy. I wanted to shave. To bathe. To not go back into the cycle of monotonous work that Mondays translate into. The gate. Behind that gate was a foreign land. A pleasant looking man with enough money to support me and him. Me. Being the hausfrau. Him the breadwinner. Strawberries, bread and spring water for breakfast. Coffee and a sweetcake later. Cigarettes smoked on a veranda or in a rear yard. Hand stitching a quilt, painting a picture, reading a novel, planting a linden or an apple tree, writing letters, curio shopping, sending tiny parcels to friends, all of it was beyond the gate. Freedom. He saw some form of enslavement. I saw all sorts of freedom. He pressed the chilly refilled glass into my hand. I studied him as he took his seat again. He pulled out a pack of Cartier cigarettes and an ashtray from the end table drawer. I instinctively reached for my own cigarettes. We studied each other as we lit up, seemingly curious about each other's habitual rituals with tobacco.

"I get it," I said.

"What's that?"

"It's easy for you to look through the gate. You see something that's possibly a negative to you. Yuppie climbing, white collar life."

"What do you see?"

"Freedoms. Freedoms that I don't have."

"Freedoms? Or fantasies?"

"Freedoms."

"Expound."

"Freedom of time. Time for myself and someone else. Time to be spent in the pursuit of growth. Your normal Joe and Josephine don't have this luxury. Most of us are living our lives living in Hell on Earth."

A broad, wry smile crept onto his face. "I like that."

"That most of us are living in Hell on Earth?"

"That you see this . . . point in time as your Hell."

"Well, I do. And, speaking of Hell, I have to go to work tomorrow. I need to find my charge and see what he's planning on doing. Five-forty-five in the a.m. doesn't sneak up on you, it leaps out on to you like Kali on a paramour."

I had to set my glass down to use my hands and arms to lift me up out of the weird chair. He remained seated, his body relaxed and spread out like dripping water colours. Sensual. Still . . . I said good-night. He nodded.

Out in the hall I rapped on Peter and Paul's door. No answer. I hadn't heard them creep out as I usually did. They never really crept out, they unintentionally made enough noise to rival the city's own thumping drone. Maybe they'd all fallen asleep. Heat does tend to make one drowsy whenever a place to rest offers itself. I went into my apartment, jotted a note to them, to Jeremy to inform them that I was going to bed and to call if Jeremy needed to crash at my place again. I tacked the note to my door.

*****

A phantom Jeremy slept soundly next to me in the darkness. I could see the contours of his silhouette tangled in the sheet and buried into the pillow. While I'd been dutiful to the point of obsession at going to the gym four to five days a week, no amount of work seemed to have much affect on the soft layer of fat that seemed to be growing around my stomach. An acquaintance who worked as a trainer at my gym had guided, poked and prodded my abdominal exercise routine. I had fine, fit muscle tone – under the layer of fat. That human butter would only go away through strict dieting. While I wasn't an obsessive over-eater, I did like to indulge now and then. Ice cream and donuts being the worst offenders. Plain chocolate was safest for me. Rationed, that is. Actually fruits were safest, but they didn't hold the same appeal, so they weren't even in the category of choices as far as I was concerned. The fat, though, was an issue for me. I liked men with a bit of a gut. There seemed to be security in knowing they had a similar fault. However, skinnyboy bodies weren't en vogue. Body beautiful was the mainstay. Create an object to be desired. Rather contrary in this time when AIDS was popping up in every other headline and tabloid article.There's death in sex, men. Abstain. Survival tells you to abstain. The counter-culture makes it difficult by having you channel those pent-up energies into constructing a body worthy of being put on display at the Metropolitan Museum. Jeremy did have such a figure. Total taboo. Let the image of his silhouette diffuse into the night. Let restive thoughts fill the void. Sleep. Sleep for tomorrow. Sleep for the strength to continue on the treadmill of life. Sleep to function. Find your function. Perform your function. Perform it as days roll into nights into days into nights until you're finally released from it all. Sleep for tomorrow.

*****

Jesus, Krishna and Mohammed were sitting around a Victorian parlour sipping a diluted red wine from Waterford goblets. Honeycakes sat untouched on a delicate porcelain plate. However, in-between sips, they all were popping chocolate coated roasted coffee beans. There was no topical debate on religion, no pointed commentaries on the fate of mankind. They talked about gardens, about hot weather, about poorly made sandals. Three people engaged in day to day topics. Simplicity. That was what life was about. The pure simplicity of an exchange of ideas on improving little things in life.

I remembered only the image of these three and their brief snippets of dialogue when I awoke all sticky and pasty in my bed. Soft, early morning light already flooded the room.The one salvation about having to go to work was that the building was air conditioned. As I showered and dressed I thought about Jeremy, wondering where he was going to end up by day's end. I tossed back the sheets on the bed, then headed out, noting my note still stuck to the door. I pulled it down and shoved it in my pocket as I left.

*****

Work is work. I sat at a desk in a large lobby, flanked by three offices. One for the Departmental Chair for the Performance Studies Department, one for the Administrative Assistant and one for the Administrative Aide – the latter two being my immediate supervisors. Gerald, the Aide, was in charge of me. He was funny. Kind of tall, kind of lanky, only a couple of months older than me. He was a bit lost like the rest of us, his talent for music going untapped at the time. This was proving not to be the decade to be associated with the Arts. Still, he persisted in his ways, getting singing gigs, and small shows whenever the opportunity arose. This was what was great about Gerald. He could identify. While he did do his damndest to do a good job for the Department, he understood that there was more to life. Neither of us were quite fit for corporate America, I felt. Anyhow, we had our squabbles now and then but they were usually about mundane things, like me being completely anal expulsive and him being very anal retentive. As long as everything functioned and ran smoothly, I saw no need for streamlined housekeeping. He liked tidiness and orderly detail. I could barely keep my shirt tail tucked in for an hour at a time. He could put on a crisp, starched shirt in the morning and will it to remain so until he removed it at night. While I liked cleanliness, I was the type who'd shove everything off of my desk onto the floor, scrub it down, then toss everything back onto it with a pitchfork.

The job itself, however, was becoming too routine. While there's a little comfort in that, it can prove to be tedious after too long. I wanted change, but didn't want change because there's always that fear factor that comes to light when one starts a new job. What if I don't cut it? What if they can me after one month? What if I find I hate it more than what I'm doing now? This kept me glued in my chair, though I did peruse the tradepapers for possible jobs in the film industry. Perhaps as an assistant. I'd done an internship or two with some larger companies while in school, these companies hereto unnamed for they were both wonderful and frightening experiences. My saving grace was knowing that since I wasn't being paid to do these jobs, no one could really get too mad at me for any errors made, nor threaten me with unemployment if I didn't cut the mustard.

During the course of the day, I called Emma, but only received her answering machine. I called Peter and Paul, expecting either or both of them to be home, but to no avail. So, I put in my time, checked out and headed home again, wondering if this life was ever going to lift out of its day to day rut.

As I exited the 725 building on Broadway, I ran into an ex-boyfriend of mine from Los Angeles. Pure happenstance. Things like that often, well not that often but often enough, happened to me in New York. There he was, Michael, with his big doe eyes. He'd been upstate visiting family and had come down to this neck of the woods to inquire about Graduate School. He still looked good. Bitch. He invited me to coffee with other friends he was hooking up with. A few of the names I remembered.

*****

Michael and the others chatted blithely away as we all sipped espresso and other dense, coffee drinks. I found myself glued to a young woman named Casey. I'd only met her a few times while we were Undergraduates. She had been two years behind me. She was working as a stage manager for a theatre company in the city but was looking to move on with any show that was a national tour. She mentioned that Michael had mentioned briefly to her as we all gathered to take our seats that he thought I seemed much more fit and centred than I'd been just a few years back. I said it was the city, it was the gym, which I still had to go to that evening, and getting older.I mentioned something in passing about being pointed onto a quest, of sorts, for growth by an old friend of mine and her uncle.

"Lisa Canton?" she asked.

"Yeah. Actually she sort of directed me to her uncle who pointed me in a direction."

"Carl," she said.

"Do you know everybody?"

"I met Carl at one of his lectures some time back. I'd gone to it to get some understanding."

"Of?"

"The path I was being directed toward," she said. The others were engrossed in their own conversations. Casey seemed to make a silent note of what was going on at the table, then continued. "I was never really into religion or metaphysics or anything. Just into the day to day struggle of getting by and getting what I wanted. One of my old roommates at college moved back home for the summer when we graduated. She asked me to store some of her stuff. No big deal. The summer came and went. The fall, then come the winter, I was offered a job out here. I tried to find her to get an address to ship her junk back to her, but she'd disappeared. I sorted through the boxes, trying to discern what I should save for her, when I found this box full of candles and tarot cards and crystals and stuff. I thought she was into witchcraft or something. Anyway, I found this small crystal ball, more like a huge marble, and sat staring at it one night.Then wham! I started seeing things in it. Weird, huh?"

"Depends on what you saw."

"Faces. Some I recognised. Some I didn't. I know I saw your face and Michael's, which was weird to me 'cause I hadn't seen you since you'd graduated. Anyway, I'd also seen the face of some man. I later saw his face in some small New Age newspaper some time later. That's how I happened on Carl and his lecture."

"Kinda like being introduced to your first grade shaman, wasn't it."

She laughed. "Interesting analogy. He helped direct me to people and tools to develop what had been born in me that day. A certain amount of instant psychic awareness. I didn't get very far staring into crystal balls, though. For me, it was too hard to interpret vague images. Tried runes and other things 'til I settled on the tarot. The cards have much more symbolic imagery."

I wanted to continue with the conversation, but Michael interrupted everyone to suggest we all go to some obscure off-off Broadway show. Tickets were only fifteen bucks. The show was bound for Broadway, and gee, it would've been nice, but the coffee drink and tip had already set me back six bucks and I still had to get to the gym. Casey and I exchanged numbers. I thanked Michael, said my good-byes and left to get on with my day to day.

*****

The gym had been crowded, the mass of sweaty bodies coupled with the lack of air-conditioning, made the whole ordeal very time consuming and laborious. I didn't get home until 9.30 that night. The apartment was its usual muggy self. There were only two messages on the machine. One from Emma returning my call. Jeremy had contacted her and amends had been made. The second call was from Jeremy. He sounded distant. Said he'd check back in with me soon and thanks for helping. That was it. I erased both, thinking I was erasing yet another brief encounter between strangers.

I thought about taking a shower, but settled for washing my face and dowsing my hair with tepid water. I could stand my own musky scent for an evening. I stretched out on my bed with one of the many books I was inclined to buy but too lazy to read. This was a quiet night, a perfect night to slip into a void by myself.

*****

I was walking through the desert, treading softly on the sand. The dunes seemed endless, yet I persevered without sweat, without thirst. I kept hearing whispers of distant laughter. Somewhere ahead in the vastness of space and time there was a party going on. Curiosity made my pace steady.

Way up ahead on a blindingly white dune, a faint shadow appeared. Small, it seemed, yet graceful like a bird of prey in flight. I shielded my squinting eyes with my hand and gazed upward, into the yellow-white sky. I glimpsed a sight of something flying, its definition obfuscated by refracted rays of light. The creature soared, flying with ease toward the laughter. At least it wasn't a buzzard waiting to lay waste to my carcass, leaving my bones to bleach dental white then to dissolve into the sand to be one with time forever.

As I crested another dune, I saw the source. At the top of that dune I stood on the edge of time, looking down a steep cliff, separated from the valley below by an abyss of fragmented space. Black, cosmic space, alive with stars and planets and asteroids hurtling lazily toward unspecified destinations. That valley below rotated slowly, like a carousel, revealing what truly seemed to be that rain-maker's magic. Verdant and beautiful. Perhaps too beautiful. Manufactured. Like a movie set. Many sets. Each akin to a carousel animal, distinct and different. As the valley turned, I saw Jesus, Krishna and Mohammed once again, laughing and singing as they worked together to replant an aging, dying fig tree near a small body of water. They worked unaware of me, unaware of the spin of the carousel, where I saw myself in a strange representation of a night-club, sitting at a table, talking with Michael, my former doe eyed ex. An image out of memory. We'd chanced upon each other that night, some years back. A night like many back then full of confusion and pain and pursuit of a lover I never fully captured. I wanted to listen in, to hear echoes of a distant conversation, but the carousel continued to turn. Casey and I were somewhere in Central Park, seated near a tree. Colourful tarot cards set out between us. Silence though. This was an image frozen, waiting for the director's cue. This, too, came and went, as various scenes, some animated, some frozen,drifted by me. Myself and Rex, a young man who at one time had fuelled my passions and pains, making love completely in the confines of my old bedroom. My big, fanciful dragon, all bright and aglow like gems in firelight, playing with children all caught up in inventive imagination. Myself, years back, beaten and alone on a beach. Emma standing on a corner, peering into the night. Lisa. Beautiful Lisa in a rose garden watching the buds bloom in early morning light. She looked at me and smiled. At least I felt she was looking at me. Probably at a distant me, locked somewhere with her in that time past. Me, again, arriving in New York City, stepping out from the cab overwhelmed and excited once again with new beginnings. Lisa, Carl and Casey atop the mighty dragon's back, lifting off and waving to no one, to everyone. The carousel picked up speed, moving the images like a slide show, the effect a bit dizzying, finally coming to a halt once again on Jesus, Krishna and Mohammed, all sitting in lawn chairs in the shade of that ancient fig tree now wondrously huge, brilliantly alive and laden with fruit. They chatted about gardens and sipped iced tea, unaware of the bodies flanking them. All of them. The mighty dragon at centre stage, the ensemble of players lined up on either side of him as if awaiting a curtain call. They all stared at me, blankly. Once again the spin of the carousel kicked in, the valley becoming a blur of green whizzing by as this stage unscrewed itself from the abyss of space and lifted off, up, ascending into the heavens.

I panicked at being left behind. I reached out and called to this cast. John Wilhelm's voice rang out.

"Ticket?"

I turned. There at the edge of time and space was John Wilhelm standing behind a childish, colourful ticket booth. "A ticket!" I wailed.

"Only one penny," he said as he held a solitary slip of silvery gold.

I was no longer in my own clothes, but instead in a pocketless tunic, running my hands up and down myself in a frantic search for one red cent. Nothing. Complete abandon. John Wilhelm shrugged emphatically and simply vanished. He and his booth and the ticket no longer an option for me. The abyss of cosmic sea was swallowed whole by a vast expanse of desert. More desert. I suddenly felt claustrophobic, as if locked away inside a coffin. I shut my eyes and sunk to my knees, silently pleading with the unseen jailer for an exit. I felt popping in my body, like bursts of static electricity, then a pressure, as if two gigantic, invisible hands gently pressed my whole body between mighty palms. I opened my eyes. There, before me, suspended in the air, was an old, weathered garden gate. I stood and slowly approached it. As I set my hand atop it and swung it open, I awoke, still, clammy and calm in my bed.

There was that flux that comes upon awakening from a vivid dream. Which is reality? This time and space or the time and space occupied by the dream? I quickly fumbled in the darkness for the lamp. The soft light illuminated secure, familiar and very concrete surroundings. My bladder was straining. I stumbled on somewhat numb legs to the toilet. The urine flushed out swiftly, blasting the water in the commode. Dizziness. The room dimmed briefly. I steadied myself for a moment against the wall, feeling the tackiness of the enamel paint. Quiet. I turned on the tap and rinsed my face and head in the basin. The day-glo numbers on my watch shot out the time. It was three in the morning.

*****

There wasn't much to eat in my poor, old refrigerator. Apples. Some cheese that still hadn't spoiled. I also had a few slices of bread, an almost empty jar of peanut butter and some yet unspoiled milk. I nibbled on an apple and a wedge of cheese. While they weren't satisfying, they filled the void in my stomach and levelled my head a bit. I wasn't sleepy. I rested on the bed once again, the night air a bit cooler than it had been in weeks. I turned my attention back to the book and read for an hour or so until my eyelids grew heavy and I drifted off to sleep again.

*****

Tuesday rolled into Wednesday, into Thursday, into Friday and I hadn't seen nor heard from Paul, Peter or Jeremy. Emma had left me another message inviting me to join her at the movies on Thursday night, but I called her machine back and begged off with some half-truthful excuse. I had passed John Wilhelm in the stairway Thursday morning as I was on my way out to work. In a nutshell of a conversation, I gathered he was completely absorbed in some art show he was working on at some obscure gallery in SoHo. It was one of those weeks when nobody called. No parents, no friends, nobody.

Friday night, after the gym, I returned home to find Peter and Paul huddled in a corner in front of our brown stone engaged in a very low, yet very heated argument. I thought it best to ignore them and sequester myself in my shoe box. While they often had insignificant disagreements, past experience had taught me to steer clear when they both seemed to be boiling over. I'd no sooner stuck my key in the lock when Peter called to me.

"What?" I said.

"Your friend's a lying sack of shit, that's what!" he screeched. I just stood there, a bit dumfounded.

Paul interceded. "Why're you yelling at him? You're mad at me!"

"If he hadn't brought that skank back here, none of this would've happened!" Peter spat as he flew past me into the building, literally ripping my key out of the lock. We heard him bound up the stairs. Their apartment door slammed hard. I just looked at Paul who was flush with anger and pain.

"It's his own fucking fault," Paul muttered as he plopped down on the stoop. I fished around for my cigarettes and offered him one. He took it absently. He expelled plumes of smoke like a snorting, pissed off dragon. His scarlet cheeks fell ashen as tears flowed freely. No heaving sobs. Just quiet tears. He didn't look at me. "Your friend Jeremy's not so straight,"he said.

The who, what, where and why weren't known to me, but I got it. "You slept with Jeremy?" I said cautiously.

"Last Sunday, when you were out, we got stoned with Jeremy," he began. "Saw the note you'd stuck on the door, so he crashed with us. It was fine. He was funny. Cooked dinner, ya know? We slept late the next morning. He woke up first an' called some friends of his. To cut to the chase, we got invited up to some guy's house near Sleepy Hollow. Nice, nice house. The guy who owned it wasn't there, but others were. Weird bunch of people. We checked in for the week, getting high, lounging by the pool, talkin' about everything an' nothing. People were screwing all over the fucking place. I was getting very turned on. So was Peter. Still, no matter how fucked up we were, he still kept his distance from me. The best he could do was some voyeuristic crap, with the two of us just jacking off while watching guys and chicks get it on wherever . . ." He took another deep drag from the butt. "We watched Jeremy get really sleazy with some Sheila chick over in a side yard beneath our window."

"Sheila . . .?" I said.

He didn't hear the comment. "They knew we were watching, so they put on a really fucking raunchy show. Peter had eaten a mushroom. He was completely raging, beating his meat in front of the window. Anyhow, the show ended. A few minutes later Jeremy was at our door, all coked up. I'd only taken a quarter of a mushroom cap so I was still sorta aware of it all . . ."

"What all?"

"Peter sat on the window sill. I was on the bed. I spread my legs. Jeremy sort of smiled, sort of sneered at Peter, then got on the bed with me and shoved his cock in my mouth. We were all fucked up. I needed physical contact. We did some heavy duty fucking there in front of Peter. I remember catching sight of him now and then, just sitting there, masturbating slowly with this weird, hard look on his face. Jeremy shot his load all over me and left. I continued to pump my cock and stare at Peter. He finally came over to me, shot his wad on me, then spat on me and locked himself in the bathroom for the rest of the night."

"Now he's pissed off . . ." I said.

"Fuck'im," he said as he flicked the cigarette butt out onto the sidewalk. "That was last night. We didn't speak until we got back here. He says he's moving out."

"So, it's my fault. It's your fault. But, none of this is his fault?"

"That's the way he wants to play, fine."

I wanted to ask where Jeremy was at the moment, but thought better against it. "He'll come 'round," I said.

"I'm tired of it. I'm not dead. I'm alive, I'm human, I have needs, too."

"Now you're sounding as pig headed as Peter. What're you gonna do, dump your years together? Eradicate them?"

He sighed and wiped his eyes with the back of his hand. "Bad judgement. That's all it was." He stood up, gave my shoulder a pat and went inside. I just sat there, smoked another cigarette and stared at the people filtering by. The scenery seemed to never change. I would be surprised if Jeremy came skulking back. Surely he'd have known I would've heard about this incident. Time passed. A few more cigarettes were smoked. Twilight ebbed into the scene. Another Friday night in the city and me without much of anything to do.

A cab pulled up at curbside. John Wilhelm climbed out. He was smiling. The cab drove off as he gamboled along the walk then parked his rear next to me. He counted the cigarette butts.

"Problems?" he said.

"Just a need for a general anaesthetic," I said.

"Like a drink?"

I'd forgotten that I'd mentioned my sobriety to him. "No. Like a week in the country without any people around."

"You wanna be left alone?" he asked.

"I wasn't making a reference to you," I said. "Just everything in general."

"Got any plans tonight?"

"Zip."

"I got a show going on tonight at eight. Come with me. There'll be other artists showing, too."

It was an offer. I took him up on the invitation. We headed inside, him disappearing into his apartment, me into mine. The message light blinked fast and furiously on my answering machine. Jeremy's voice on the first four calls. All hang-ups thereafter. He really sounded distraught and confused. I didn't want to call him back, but I would've, had he left me a phone number. I thought about calling Emma. But what if he wasn't there? She'd make inquiries. Could I be deceptive? Keep her from worrying again? I wished I'd understood their relationship. Maybe they didn't understand it themselves. I decided it was best to let them call me again, rather than me sticking my nose into anything I didn't really understand.

*****

I didn't quite understand the art show or shows. They were all spacial artists, like John Wilhelm. His was a bit odd, but a bit intriguing. An entire room wherein all the furnishings were depicted by string outlines. The strings had differing colours, depending on the type of furniture. End tables, a coffee table, a television were all black string. Some pieces were starched into stiff formation forming the base frameworks, such as the oval of a table top. These were suspended by invisible nylon threads stapled into the ceiling. Downward shapes, such as table legs, were tied to the suspended forms then stapled to the floor. Cheaply made art. Some string, a staple gun and some watercolours. I got it, yet didn't get it. It was transient. Once the display was taken down, there wasn't much left. Oh well. Other shows were just as bizarre. One room was almost filled to capacity with stuffed, plastic garbage bags. Another had frames of cubes, shrinking in size as they moved inward to the centre, rather like layers of an onion. At the core was a popsicle stick relief of a three, three being a symbol for the mathematical term 'cubed'. Call me unenlightened, label me dense, but I didn't see the point to this form of art. On any given day, I could see authentic heaps of trash bags on almost any given corner in the city. Bags complete with their own aromas and insects. John Wilhelm was ecstatic. His work was being very well received, as if it were almost recherche. I sipped cider, he sipped champagne as we made our rounds, meeting and greeting folks I was sure I'd never ever see again. One thing about John, he was always adamant about introducing me to everyone. That was nice, though not necessary in my mind for I had little to say to anyone. This wasn't my kind of art.

We left the party with a lesbian couple, M'greet and Susan, to share a cab ride to some party being held in a West Village warehouse. The entire ride, M'greet and John talked about space while Susan and I were each jammed into the cab's passenger doors, struggling for elbow room. I managed to twist my shoulders to free my pinned arms a bit. I noticed that it was already ten minutes to midnight. I really wanted to go home. Still, it was his night. He'd chosen me to invite along to share this triumph with, so who was I to rain on his parade. Maybe I could get some coffee or strong tea to keep me awake. Susan didn't seem to be enjoying this much, either. Her head was resting on the window, her yawns fogging the glass.

The warehouse, the whole waterside neighbourhood, seemed very, very remote. As dead as Wall Street at six a.m. on a Sunday morning. We climbed out of the cab. M'greet instinctively led the way through an almost invisible metal door, down a long, dark corridor to a freight elevator. I could faintly hear the chords of some sort of baroque music. Chords similar to the ones our detached neighbour Julie played on her saws and cans.

The elevator landed and we spilled out into a room with the most eclectic confab of bodies I'd seen in years. Severe, monied, poor, pasty, tanned, whatever could describe someone was covered in this mix. M'greet pulled Susan along to join some rather anaemic looking woman, tossing good-byes to John and me as they went. I studied John who studied the faces in the crowd. It was quite obvious he was looking for someone and not spotting him or her. A rather boorish looking man came up to us and whisked John away into a small enclave with spotty chat about his work being 'to die for'. I remained by the elevator, peering through cigarette and pot haze, wishing I'd just stayed home. My name was called. My full name. It was Julie. Winsome, waifish Julie of the saws. As slender as a willow sapling, as white as bleached flour she was. Quite a sight with her long, straight hair dyed crayon black and her black lipstick and kohl lined eyes. She preferred to call people by their full names to eradicate any confusion in a crowd.

"Hello, Julie."

"Happenstance, isn't it," she said as she sipped from a glass of pale chablis.

"Your music?" I said, referring to the composition that leaked out from small speakers.

"There was supposed to be an alternative music producer here tonight," she said. "Naturally he was nothing more than a wannabe. Typical."

"No deal."

"Don't be glib."

"Haven't seen you around the building for a while," I said.

"I was having a lesbian affair. Nice, but not me, you know?"

"I can understand that," I said.

She pointed to John Wilhelm. "Isn't he the one who moved into our building?" I nodded. "He's got a certain magnetism," she continued as she eyed him between sips.

"Is he gay?"

I shrugged. "Says he's divorced." She cocked an eyebrow inquisitively. "I don't really know his story," I said. "He's attractive, but I don't see any . . . sensuality? Sex appeal?"

"He's not auditioning for a toothpaste commercial," she said with a smile.

"Might work. You two, I mean."

"Too bad I have to go to Boston tomorrow morning," she said as she handed me her glass and fished a red cigarette from her purse. "Light?"

I lit her smoke for her, trying to picture gigantic John and diminutive Julie rocking the bedsprings. He'd think nothing more of it once the event transpired. He'd go about his day-to-day business while she became introspective, moody and possibly suicidal. A great mix. Opposite polarities.

"He'd make me suicidal," she blurted out softly. "Fuck men. Fuck women. Fuck anything and everything."

"Except music."

"That's most fucked sometimes. So little room in this country for expansive arts. Pursuing a vision is like masturbating with a piece of cactus."

"There are some who would enjoy that."

"Are you going home? Want to share a cab?" she said.

I did want to. I made my apologies to John who was so enraptured with the praise and fawning he was receiving that he didn't seem to take note of the point that I was leaving. Julie and I slipped out very unnoticed.

We had to walk to Christopher and Seventh to catch a cab. Near Sheridan Square where I'd met Emma. Julie and I didn't talk much about anything of merit. Glib talk underscored with pointed comments. The cab deposited us at our brownstone and we disappeared into separate apartments and back to our separate lives.

I stripped and stretched out on my bed, staring into the void of darkness. Night wrapped about me like a fichu yet I was unable to sleep. I felt something inside me. Tapping slightly, intermittently. Something so long buried that I'd negated it ever having existed. It was a pang, an element of memory of emotion from a time, only a few years back, when I could feel the pains of wanting, longing, desire, even love. But that was ridiculous. Sobriety and calm had entered my life some time back, eliminating my obsessions and fixations and chaotic thoughts and actions. I'd moved from an arena of active participation to the bleachers of passive observation. A safe place to be. Perhaps I misinterpreted the feeling. Perhaps I was just horny, needing a sexual fix to tranquilise me as a Quaalude once did. It had been some time, many months in fact,since I'd experienced carnal bliss. So much wasn't understood about this virus, this AIDS thing that gripped gay life with the threat of death. Many called it many things. Through abstinence, I'd ignored it, save for knowing that Peter held it within him. Still, what risks could I take – would I take – to find someone for myself? My old mind-set leached through as I slipped out of bed and into my clothes. It felt odd to be so compelled to do what the rational mind said not to do.

Out on the street, I headed up Second Avenue, skirting hawkers of drugs and transients, and made my way to Fourteenth Street. Near that very corner, where I'd chanced upon Jeremy only days before, was a porn house. Though I'd walked by it many times, never quite seeing the frustrated faces that snuck out of it with bent heads and fists buried in pockets, I had never peered inside. It was open to the street. Vulnerable. I'd always remained closed. Protected.

*****

The minute I set foot inside, the dim lighting, the smell of cigarette smoke and sex, my mind flashed back years to my life in Los Angeles. Drug spent and hell bent on destruction. Compelled to investigate, I stepped through the curtained archway, into the theatre space. Flickering, pale light drew me in.

Men lined the aisle wall, so many sentient mannequins, their eyes watching me as I walked past to an empty seat that squeaked low as I sat down. I fixed my sight on the screen – a scratchy print of a ten year old film loomed on the slightly warped screen. Bad music score. Shaky filming. An old super 8 loop of three guys sucking and fucking each other in a rather haphazard fashion, conscious of the camera being able to get tight shots of their animalistic actions. The film was schlock. A poorly made fuck film. While I stared at the screen, I was keenly aware of men filtering down the darkened aisle then through an open doorway marked EXIT. I thought perhaps there was some cloistered back corner, a patch of ground fenced in, or a private section of alleyway where they found privacy to trick with each other. I tried to dredge up arousal. My own. My cock remained limp. I let my eyes roam, trying to find some inspiration in the form of a man. The dimness fought me. Still, compelled more by instinct than desire, I shifted from my seat to the aisle, never looking at anyone as I made my way to that exit.

Blackness blinded me. I could hear but could not see the zipping of zippers, the rustle of pants being tugged down or up, the dull clinking of change in pockets, the heavy breathing, the low slurping and sucking and other sounds of pleasure. I sensed a presence behind me. Cigarette breath snorted softly on my neck as large hands and arms clasped gently about me, massaging my chest, making their way down to my crotch. The man pressed into me, guiding me deeper into the room. As my eyes adjusted to the darkness, I caught sight of him. Okay. Hard looking. He slipped around me on bending knees, his hands slipping up the legs of my shorts, finding me. Me. Growing hard quickly. He swallowed my cock, slamming his chin, his nose, into my pelvis. It felt good. He sucked hard, with a purpose – to bring me to climax and drain me. I didn't want to come in his mouth. I tried to push him back, but another man insinuated himself on us, sandwiching me between himself and the other. It didn't take all that long. It'd been forever since I'd had sex with anyone. My penis slowly deflated in his mouth. He squeezed the shaft, my balls at the base and ran his raspy tongue all over. The other man reached under my shirt and squeezed my nipples, his mouth and tongue manoeuvring to find mine. I relented, giving way to suppressed needs. We kissed hard. Whiskers sanding whiskers, scraping flesh from tongue and cheek. Teeth chewing lips, biting tongues gently as we swallowed each other. A hand slide my shorts down, exposing my ass to his probing fingers, to his own exposed, slick, hard cock. I wanted to get fucked then and there, in view of everyone who cared to look. I wanted to, but I didn't. I had a flash. Of what, I wasn't sure. I pulled away from him, pulled up my shorts, gave his cock a squeeze and left. Seven dollars. That's what I'd paid to get into the pornhouse. Seven dollars for a blow job.

I quietly left the porn house, aware of the traffic, aware of the many eyes that were possibly getting a glimpse of me fleeing the scene of this crime. I walked and walked quickly the blocks back to the brownstone.

*****

As I scoured myself in the shower, I tried to rationalise my action. To forgive myself for being so desperate. It was there and then that I got a glimmer of understanding about what was transpiring. I'd come to New York as a new beginning. However, somewhere along the way, I lost track of finding my own story and a logical or illogical ending. One doesn't begin a quest of any sort without stopping. Thc original purpose becomes lost; the original action aborted. However, was I ignoring my quest, or some other purpose already defined and even, perhaps, executed by my higher self? I had been akin to a jackal at one time. Action was born out of fear. Fear bred inaction. Inaction did not breed courage – the courage to continue with the journey through life, seeking answers to questions yet to be asked.

The dreams, queer that they were, were beginning to feel right, though I could analyse them until doomsday and propose more interpretations to myself than would probably ever be valid. Casey flashed in my mind. Casey.

Someone with a purpose, it seemed. Someone with possible tools to guide me along as my friend Lisa had done some years before.

*****

I remembered no dreams the following morning. A bit disconcerting. Especially since I'd armed myself with a pen and note pad at the ready to take notes. It was early. Too early to pick up the phone and dial Casey. Too early to dial up anyone I knew. I just lay in bed, thinking about where this journey in life was taking me. I did this until stomach rumblings forced me up and out of bed and out the door to the small Korean owned market a few blocks away.

*****

Strawberries. Deep red. Large. Almost at the point of rotting. Their fragrance alone prompted me to purchase them and a couple of croissants. A beautiful breakfast by any standard. I also picked up a bottle of cold water then headed out with my bag of goods. I started toward home, but the early morning air was so fresh for a change that I walked over to Washington Square Park. As I neared the park, I veered into one of the NYU buildings to rinse the basket of berries in a water fountain and to purloin some paper towels from the men's room, then continued on to an unoccupied bench.

As I nibbled I watched the early morning rituals of vagrants, of joggers, of walkers, of the pigeons and squirrels. No one disturbed this time for me. Sitting and observing was an awesome sort of power. The questions it raised. What connection, if any, did I have with these people, these strangers who filled the grounds before me. There are so very many people in this world. What plan of fate was it that drew specific ones together? Was there a plan at all? Random chance? Was something slipping by me that I was completely unaware of? Probably. Men walk with eyes closed even when they're wide open. Men stick their fingers into so many pies around them that they're only left with stumps for hands to work with. I realised as I tossed my trash into the waste receptacle that I needed to jumpstart my life again. How, I didn't know.

Walking home, I wanted a vision. To be struck dumb full of insight into the greater purpose of it all. No thunderbolts came, though. Just images of recent events. Jeremy stuck in my mind.What demons were eating at him? Shredding him. Helping him shred others. Had I seen the same demon once before? It was hard to reflect on my past life of chaos and deep pains with any objectivity. Oh well, I thought, whatever's meant to be will be.

I rounded my corner and caught sight of Peter and Paul sitting once again on the front stoop. They seemed calm. As my hand touched to gate, I noticed how warm and sticky it was, foretelling of another hot, humid day. I smiled at them. They both looked at me, independent, silent thoughts seemingly directed at me. There had been forgiveness. I could tell.

They scooted over, making room for my rear end to park next to them. Paul sniffed me.

"Strawberries?" he said.

"Wonderful strawberries."

He and Peter exchanged some sort of coded glance, then they both turned and smiled at me. I grinned. They gave each other a quick peck of affection. Peter leaned toward me.

"Jeremy came by looking for you," he said.

"When?"

"About a half hour ago," Paul said blandly. "He said he'd come back later." I wasn't sure whether this was good news or bad news. Especially considering what had transpired between these two and him. Paul softened with a slight smile. "What happened with us and Jeremy, well, he was just a catalyst that was maybe needed to help us confront and resolve some of our own issues."

"It's hard for me to sit in judgement on him. It's not my place since I've walked his walk before," I said.

"That was yesterday. This is today," Paul said.

"There must be something he sees in you," Peter said. "I'm not sure what, though."

"A crash pad."

"More than that," Paul said. "There was something in his eyes. Like he was scared shitless, ya know?"

"He is scared," I said. "I know that much 'cause I've been there. He's looking for solutions to problems, but in the search he takes down a few people, affecting them."

"Well, whatever the case, he's gonna be back, so be forewarned," Paul said.

I nodded and gave them a quick adios and disappeared into my box. I belly flopped onto my bed, suddenly overcome with a need for a nap. I no sooner started to snooze when there came a rap on my door. I groaned, rolled off the bed and answered the call. Jeremy stood there, looking like a mangy tom cat after losing a brawl. The welt around his left eye and cheek was already dulling rotten banana brown. Dried blood caked a slit on his lower lip.

"Paul said you'd looked scared, but not this scared."

"I asked him not to tell."

I stepped aside and let him in. He headed for my bed. I grabbed him by the arm and led him into the kitchen, parking him at the tiny table in the corner. I wetted a towel, folded it up and tossed it in the freezer, then wetted a wad of paper towels to blot his lip. The crusty scab gave way quickly. Blood trickled out from the slit. It wasn't a deep cut. I globbed some Neosporin on it, then had him press the paper towelling down on it to stop the new bleeding.

"What hit you this time?"

"Sheila's ex-boyfriend."

I pulled the folded towel from the freezer. It was a cool enough. I pressed it against the welt. "I'm not your mother, Jeremy. I don't even let old friends test my limits this much."

"I'm going back to the program. N.A."

"Being an A.A. graduate myself, I understand what you're doing. Go back. See what happens. Can't get much worse than it already has, can it?" I said. I took the paper towel from him. The lip stopped bleeding.

"Emma's not talking to me."
"Do you blame her?"
"No," he sighed.
I pressed the compress into his hand. "You know where everything is. I'm going back to my nap."

*****

I wasn't really sleeping. More like lost in deep thought and exhaustion and I wasn't even sure why I was tired. Some say it's a sign of depression. Some say you should fight the urge to sleep by getting up and going out and doing something. Do what, though? The gym? I'd already been there five days this week. Too much was too much. The museum? Too many people. Read a book? I'd fall fast asleep, defeating the purpose. Take another picnic in the park? I just didn't feel like moving at all. I felt the bed give a bit. Jeremy eased down beside me, smelling fresh, smelling wet from yet another shower. Thank God I wasn't the one paying the water bill. The one amenity of life the city insisted building owners pay. I rolled over to face him. Those brownish green eyes just stared into my own. Tiny beads of perspiration lined his upper lip. His hand reached out to me, stroking my cheek, coming to rest on my arm. I slipped my hand into his and gave it a slight squeeze. Once again, he slid down and balled himself up into me. Sleep. Always sleep.

He slept. I just lay there, cradling him. Listening to him breathe. Feeling the velvety hardness of his back. Fighting old urges to release the jackal inside me. The creature that would happily feast on this vulnerable form exposed naked to me save for the short nylon running shorts that weakly guarded his most desirable delicacies. I lay back, not wanting to think about him, about desires. I lay back to distance myself a bit. My sleepy charge nestled down a bit, nuzzling his face into the soft of my belly. A hand crept quietly over my thigh, up under the leg of my shorts. Fingers crawled lightly like spiders until they came to rest on my brief clad crotch. My cock stiffened instantly in response to the probe. I was still conscious. I had the power to stop this action then and there. My history was spiced with too numerous accounts of having sex for the wrong reasons. I'd sealed up that fearful animal I harboured inside me. Sealed him up under layers of bricks. Sealed him in darkness with the child I once was but never knew. Stop it now, I thought as I felt him climb between my legs and tug at the waistbands of cotton protection. Stop it, I thought as I lifted my hips to help him free myself, as the briefs and shorts skidded down my legs and off my body. Stop it now, I insisted to myself as I felt his lips and tongue massage the head of my cock. Oh God . . .

I sat up on my elbow, my free hand cupping him under his chin. I gently eased my member from his mouth. His eyes were large and full of fear, of pain, of needing. He sat up on his knees. His own shorts were gone, revealing his offering to me. I recognised him. He was me some years back, full of apprehension. Was he wanting to give himself to me because it was what he truly wanted to do? Or was this a desperate act of ingratiation. To manipulate me. To earn himself favour and reason to call on me at any time of need in any hour? Would I regret it later?

"What's wrong?" he whispered.

"Can you tell me?"

"I want to."

"Sheila. Emma. Peter and Paul."

"Emma was different. You're different."

"I'm not Emma, though."

He just stared at me as he lowered himself back down on me. His eyes locked on mine as his lips parted and he slid his moist mouth over my shaft. I shivered. I wanted. I wanted him. I reached down to pull him up onto me, but he resisted, locked in on oral copulation. His back arched. His ass riding high in the air. His palms, his fingers kneaded hard the flesh and muscles of my thighs. My mind kept flashing signals. Stop. Stop it now. This isn't us. His head bobbed and twisted. Saliva coated my groin. My mouth watered for him. For his flesh. For the folds of foreskin rolling across my tongue, pinched by my lips. To have him swell up in my throat. To have him press between my ass cheeks and ride me hard.

I could feel myself swelling to the point of ejaculation. I sat up and bore down hard on his shoulders, easing off his resistance. My cock bounced from his mouth. A strand of spit kept us linked. He was tearing. Maybe crying. I slipped my hands under his sweating armpits and guided him up on top of me. His semi-hard dick pressed against mine. His glistening lips panting a scant few inches from my own. The one lip was still swollen, though not bleeding. The yellowish brown welt still hurt, I could tell. I felt myself tearing. It felt good. It felt foolish. He kissed me, gently. Our lips brushed against each other. Strokes on canvas. Our tongues probed, intertwined with each other's. He licked the wetness from my eyes as he let his weight come to rest on me. His heart. I could feel it beating – beating through my own chest. The butts of my palms pressed hard into his back. I felt knotted muscles give way as I plowed down to his tail bone. The hint of the rise of his ass coaxed me on. My fingers timidly felt the firmness of each buttock. The looseness of its fullness. His cock strained to the overture. Concupiscence brought the creature out from hiding in its briar patch. Its growth tugging on the hairs of my pelvic area. I slid a hand between us to feel him.His skin slightly loose along the hard shaft. A slight bit of overhang of flesh protecting his swollen cock head. I felt my sphincter relax. My sweat lubricated hole wanted to slip him inside. Instinctively my legs spread out then wrapped about his thighs. His cock slid up and down, dry humping me.

"Want it?" he breathed.

"You want it," I sighed.

He stopped and lay hard on top of me again. "I'm usually stupid," he said as his eyes tried to see beyond mine. "Don't you be stupid, too."

I thought about the night stand. He glanced over at it then back at me. I smiled, I think. His long arms fished around in the drawer and came up with a brand new box of condoms. Another casting and he found a small bottle of lubricant. While still straddling me, he eased into a latex sheath as I swabbed a bit of jellish goo on my hole and him. My hand gripped my loose briefs to quickly towel it off. We resumed. He slowly entered me, allowing me some comfort. Once all the way in, I felt I never wanted to let him out of me. Slow, steady pumping completely relaxed me. He was a kisser. I liked that. Total involvement.

Flesh suctioned against flesh as our bodies flooded the bed with sweat. Drenching sweat. Clean sweat. We meshed for hours, shifting all about the bed. I came twice without ever touching myself, without ever falling soft. His quiet panting gave way to an animalistic groan as he let loose with a few very hard, slapping thrusts and spent himself. I confess I rather missed being able to feel him shoot his load up deep inside me, but it was nonetheless extremely . . . extreme. He lowered himself on me, his head tucked under my chin, against my chest. He was still in me. We fell asleep.

*****

A hard projectile took a right turn against my head. I sat up with a start. Jeremy seemed to have been as abruptly awakened as well. I first saw the book, a large paperback, skitter across the floor, then, there in the doorway was Emma. Raging. Red. Trembling with anger. Balled up fists on twitching arms strained, wanting to rip the flesh from my form, from his form. Her eyes were fixed on not him, but me. Jeremy bounced up from the bed to confront her, shifting her focus and fury and allowing me a moment to snag my shorts.

"What the hell's with you barging in here?" he yelled. I heard a grating slap.

"You fucking, fucking son-of-fucking-bitch bastard!"she shrieked for the city and God to hear. Whappity-whappity-slap-slap-slap. Her hands, her fists flew across him like propellers chopping air, delivering the final outcome. "Fucking faggot queer fuckhead maggot! Die! I hope you die!"

Jeremy slapped her hard. Stunned silence. For a second.

Then the siren wailed a blur of obscenities that mounted into a shriek so loud, so pained, it was as if she'd been vivisected on the very spot. Her knees started to give way – Jericho falling – but she snapped to, spat on Jeremy, then turned on her heels and charged away. Jeremy stood naked and speechless in the doorway. I gently pulled him back and shut the door, locking it.

He leaned against it, slowly sinking down into a squat. He thunked the back of his head against the door a few times, venting some frustration. "Shit . . . " he sighed. I sat down next to him, took his hand in mine and gave it a feeble but reassuring squeeze. There were welts rising on his cheek, below the bruised injury. Three tiny furrows swelled up, blooming with opened capillaries."I never get it right," he muttered.

"Yes, you have."

He fixed his gaze on mine. My arm wrapped about his shoulders, then guided his head into my lap. His body flowed, nestling into me like a kid in need of impromptu security from a grandparent. We sat there like that for some time. Me, propped against the door. He on his side, drawn up into me. Brick by brick my wall was falling away once again. Pain is powerful. Is debilitating. Is healing. It's impossible to know if you're weakening or gaining strength when you feel like you're sinking in the quagmire. He was sinking. I was sinking. I felt that disconcerting tweak in my gut, in my heart. Emotions were once again running out like water through a hole in a dike. I started to cry. Quietly. He up chucked a sob of slobber, snot and tears, releasing all that had been stuffed in his own dark place. The room swam before me and I felt as if I were at the centre of a vortex. His sobs were for him. Mine for me.

We seemed to sit there for hours. It may have just been minutes. We were spent through and through. Jeremy finally picked himself up off of me. It was muggy again. I sweated innocuously from my temple, chest and armpits. He stood up, proffering his hand. I accepted his gesture and stood up.

"I think I've disrupted enough lives for twenty

lifetimes," he said to me.

"Meaning . . . "

"I'm not living in the real world."

"Who is?" I said.

"People with real jobs. With real relationships. With rents'n mortgages to pay," he muttered, coughing up some spittle. "Not me. I fuck up'n fuck up'n fuck up some more."

"How can you get it right, if you don't know what you're even trying to do?" I asked.

"I've been trying to take myself down an' I can't even do that right. Pretty pathetic, hun."

"Been there. Did that. I'm still standing."

"But what the fuck for? To spend forty years workin' for the man? To keep a roof over your head, food in your gut?"

"You've never thought to consider what you want," I said. "Have you?"

He thought for a second, then busied himself straightening out the bed covers. "I'm a waiter slash model who's not bad but not great at either job. I dropped out of college during my Junior year to take some hack job with a bad record label, thinkin' I was gonna become some young, hip A and R man. Discover bands, singers, eventually manage their superstellar careers and rake in some bucks. When that crapped out, I did the model gig, thinkin' I'd get lucky and my good looks'd land me on some sitcom or soap, but I found out I'm one shitty actor. So I think about what I'm good at. Cooking. I like to cook. But everyone wants you to have a fuckin' degree from some expensive culinary school to even become a prep cook. Came out here thinking I'd get to France. Ya know, enroll in a real culinary institution there. I was supposed to have a modelling gig in Paris for a Japanese designer. That job fell through and I was stuck here. That was the reality. That is the reality."

He stared at the bed. He'd made it neat and tidy. He finally spun around and flopped back on it like a kid too through with school. I crept up onto the bed beside him. "So, you've given up," I said.

"What about you? I mean, what do you do besides work an' live here?"

"Not much."

"So, you've given up, too?" he asked.

"I don't know that I'd call it giving up, but I came here for change. I got change. I'm not sure though if it was right for me, so until I decide on a course to follow, I lay low, out of harm's way. Hopefully."

"The clock still ticks."

"And the pages of the calendar get ripped off and tossed aside like discarded wrappers. I know." He propped himself up on his elbow and bent down and kissed me. A friendly kiss. The claw marks were swollen, the traces of blood caked brown. "What do you see when you dream, Jeremy?"

"I don't see anything."

"Everyone dreams."

"I gave it up for Lent one year. Never went back to it."

"Are they that bad?" I asked.

"Why does it matter what I dream?" he said as he rolled back flat on the bed. "Dreams get analysed. A dozen people will give you three dozen interpretations. You think about all thirty six possibilities of why yer mind's fucked up and whaddaya get? More fucked up."

"You don't discard any irrelevant information you're given, then," I said.

"My whole life has been a discard."

"Why not try listening to the little tapes in your head when they tell you to pay attention?" I said as I propped myself up on an elbow and leaned over him. "There's always some tape, some voice that creeps in that you sure as shit don't want to listen to. That's when you gotta listen and hear what it's saying."

His eyes lit with a spark. A constrained smile tried to reveal itself on his face. "Fuck you," he quipped.

"You already did that."

He sprung up abruptly and pinned me down. "What're you thinkin' about now?"

"You." My hips lifted off the bed, bucking him. As he went up, I slithered down between the bridge of his legs, coming to rest with his cock and balls whispering above my face. My tongue probed his prepuce as my lips clamped down to nurse on the fleshy fold. An addiction was immediately back in my life. Sex. All that was male, all that was him, was mine at that moment and I devoured him, feeling the silky, smoothness of his hardening penis swell up in my mouth. Wet tongue and saliva slathered lips sought out his pleasure. My pleasure. Greedy, starved appetite satiating itself. His cock, his scrotum, finally his ass. The most base, most revelled, most reviled portion of anatomy. My fingers spread his clenched cheeks, allowing me access. He trembled as my lips and tongue manipulated his hole, penetrating him, nuzzling him, needing him. Like a virgin, his resolve melted away and he eased himself down, over me, laying prone and offering up his most vulnerable, most protected piece of himself. I accepted it gratefully.

Lust? Love? Perhaps something of a mix of both. We continued to make love again and again as hours slipped by. It felt right to see it as making love. It was. Hedonistic, pornographic, rampant encounters fulfil the moment, then the parties involved can go on their separate ways, satisfied. Making love can be never ending, all absorbing. We continued until we fell asleep, entwined in each other, in the darkness.

*****

I awoke very early, very aware of the scents and sensations of our coupling. While I wanted these to remain on me, in me, I couldn't very well walk through the day looking and smelling like something that stumbled out of a bath house after a drunken frenzy of flesh. Well, I could've, but society does so frown. Jeremy was in a deep, deep sleep. Just looking at him, matted hair, battered face and all, I felt desire stirring again. Leave him be, I thought. Get on with it, sans obsession.

I luxuriated in the relaxing steam of the shower, feeling the soap and shampoo and razor scrub and scrape residue from my body, though ever listening for any faint sounds that might be stirring in the other room. I heard nothing. I felt him to still be there. This was an oddly comforting sensation. As I turned off the water, I listened again. Under the drip-drip-dripping of the faucet, I heard the slow, exhausted exhalations of a man drunk with the sandman's spell. I toweled off, went into the toilet to urinate and dry my hair. As I stared at my reflection in the mirror, I visioned through the looking glass, into John Wilhelm's abode and at that gate that hung on his wall. I'd walked through that gate, to the other side, last night. That freedom I so wanted had been made evident, even if only for a brief moment in time. I'd closed myself off from freedom. I'd constricted my life with self-imposed constraints. Freedom is found in the moment for there's nothing else. That was, should've been, the joy of childhood. Freedom in the moments. Nothing calculated, nothing planned. A simple solution.

I dressed and milled about the kitchen. I found some Bartlett pears in with the few remaining apples. I'd picked up some French bread during the week and some other odds and ends. I laid out bread, fruit and razor thin slices of ham on a plate as the tea kettle bubbled over. I poured two mugs of brewed tea. Coffee seemed a bit heavy. I balanced it all rather well, owing to years of waiting tables, and carried it in, to him. A gentle nudge and he awakened, stretching a bit, wincing a bit as he absently rubbed the sleep from the wrong side of his face, then smiling as he viewed food before him. He grabbed a pear and bit into it. Juice dribbled down his chin onto his chest. He sat up slowly, set the mugs of tea on the nightstand and moved the plate aside. He then offered his pear to me. I bit into it. Sweet, solid and wet. He took another bite, then abruptly pulled me down, half on him, half beside him. A wedge of fruit was clenched between his teeth. I bit off the exposed half. Our lips locked as the sweetmeat in separate mouths became reunited. I pulled up, off of him, swallowed, then placed the plate back before him.

"Eat something," I said. "Rumbling stomachs disturb my concentration."

"What're you thinking?"

"Whether you're a duplicitous rogue or sincere everyman,"I said.

"That's the way it is with me. There's always a question."

"Is there, though?"

"I don't want there to be one," he said as he stared up at the ceiling. "When I start out as one, I end up as the other."

"Well, I don't expect anything," I said.

"No?"

"People drift in and out of our lives everyday. I learned a long time ago not to expect anything."

He nodded slightly as he chewed up the rest of the pear. We ate quietly. When the last bit was done, I took the plate and mugs into the kitchen, giving them a cursory washing. Jeremy came up behind me at the sink, slipping his arms under mine and hugging me hard. As I turned toward him, he gave me a peck then waddled off into the tub room. Images of June and Ward Cleaver popped into my head. We were anything but their wholesome image. My Sunday morning image, sans the newspaper, had been born.

I remade the bed, almost intoxicated by the euphoriant smell of sex that lingered in the warp and woof of the sheets. Smells linger for a time, then fade as they're either washed away or bleached away by light or replaced with scents of times to come. Again, the mugginess of summer crept in through thin walls and open windows. Jeremy come out dressed in some other old garments I had lingering in the closet. Emma's claw marks were no longer swollen. Just fine lines of scabs. The welt was now a deep brown-blue, but the swelling of that wound, too, had gone down. I smiled at him. "Almost human."

He grinned. "What're you doing today?"

"I was gonna go up to Central Park, find a quiet spot and make a list of the changes I need to make in my life."

"I need to make some changes," he said. "I'm gonna go try and talk my way back into my sublet."

"What if you can't?"

"My friend up in Washington Heights has a storage space out in Brooklyn. He can get his work van and we can dump my junk into storage with his if I have to."

"First steps are all that's needed," I said.

"If I have to come back for another night . . ." he started.

"I'm not throwing you out, Jeremy. Not yet, anyhow." I picked up my backpack, then dug around in a drawer for one of my spare set of keys. I hesitated for an instant, reticent to allow him such carte blanche. Hell, I thought, he'd probably lose them before the day was out anyhow. I turned, jangling the keys before him. "Keys. Lose'em and you'll be camping out on the stoop."

He seemed puzzled for a second. "You're gonna trust me?"

"Is there cause not to?" He took the keys with a very muffled thank you. I grabbed some tokens for the subway, hiked the backpack up onto my shoulders and nodded to him. "Good luck today." I left.

*****

Maybe the subway was a mistake. Where all the mass of humanity came from on a Sunday morning was beyond me. Wall to wall, butt to crotch to nose and back again. I wasn't even sure that the sweat on my body was my own or someone else's dripping all over me. I unloaded at 72nd or 77th Streets. I knew it was the Seventies at any rate. I had to get out of the underground broiler. The daylight seemed cool by comparison. I walked the blocks, stopping briefly in a market for a bottle of water, then finally trekked into the park. So much cooler beneath the shade of trees. I meandered through it, toward the West Side in the Eighties, to the lake where the ducks chattered and scrounged for food. I took a seat in a quiet area, on a covered bench at the water's edge. Behind me, through the trees, I could see the top of the Dakota, John Lennon's home. I wondered what his view was like.

I set the bottle of water beside me then pulled out a notebook. Lists didn't come easily. I leaned back, lit a cigarette and watched the ducks paddle around, bobbing occasionally under the surface of the lake in search of a tasty meal. I crushed the butt and continued to stare out over the water. Suddenly this wiry little dog leapt into my lap, frantically washing my face with doggy kisses. I caught her up in my hands and held her up. Sharkey.

"Well, well, well," came the voice. I turned. Carron stood there, red hair and summer dress flowing in the slight breeze. A leash dangled from her wrist. "Sharkey knew there was something rotten to roll around in out here."

"Hey, hey," I smiled. "Come and collect your charge."

She took Sharkey from me, reattaching her leash, then sat by me. Sharkey immediately leapt back up into my lap and nestled down. "She never was very discriminating," Carron said.

"Of course not. Look at who her Master is."

"What do you think you're doing coming up into my neighbourhood and not stopping by?"

"I should've known better than to try. There's radar up here in nosebleed territory."

"Village snob."

"I try," I said.

"So, what are you doing way up here?"

"Thinking about change."

"You're not moving back to L.A., are you?"

"Maybe," I said. "Maybe, too, I just need someplace else."

"Pooh," she purred. "You love New York."

"But I'm not doing anything."

"You didn't do anything in L.A., or Fresno, or Newport or Santa Cruz . . ." she began.

"Okay, okay."

"Nobody really does anything in New York, either. I mean, most nobody. Most are making money and spending it, or trying to make it and still spending it. Cities are exciting places, but they're hard, especially if you're flat broke and don't have a rich Uncle Maurie and Aunt Clara who'll subsidise you. Besides, this notion's got to do with something. You're one of those people I know most resistant to change."

She allowed me to spend the next hour or so succinctly

recounting my experiences with Jeremy, with the notions of John Wilhelm and his bizarre wooden gate, with the general stagnation I'd been feeling since I'd matriculated with my wonderfully useless Master's Degree. When I finished, as if on cue, Sharkey got up and padded over into her lap.

She sat for a moment, studying the pup who snorted into a relaxed snooze. "What would you like to do?" she asked simply. "I don't mean to do as a means to an end, like amassing great wealth and notoriety, or to be some pseudo-productive member of society, or any of that. Just, what is it you want to do? What is your want?"

"To just read, write, sketch, sew, fix dinner, clean house, iron clothes . . ." I said.

"So, you want to be a housewife, of sorts, free of financial responsibilities. Well, unless you marry rich, you can't. So, why not pursue the creative ends in your off hours? See where they lead you."

"I thought about that. I made some attempts. But, every time I start to embark on some endeavour, time becomes constricted. Project conclusions seem like they're never going to arrive, you know."

"I think you should hang around that John Wilhelm a bit more," she said. "He's got the right vision. Even if his art doesn't make sense to you or to anyone, he's getting it looked at. You can do it, too. You've just got a few extra flights of stairs to climb to get there. Pick up something you started to do but didn't finish it and finish it," she said.

"You insist on making things sound simple, don't you."

"That's what I'm here for," she said. "I've got to get back and make myself dazzling and festive for a dinner party tonight." She gave me a peck as she stood and put a somewhat groggy Sharkey on the ground. "I'll be back in around nine if you want to call."

We tossed good-byes. She and Sharkey disappeared out on to the city streets. I glanced at the ducks who were still doing what they'd been doing forever. I took up the notebook and my pen and stared hard at the blank page. Finally, the pen moved.

*****

It took awhile to dig the box out of my cramped closet, but I did find it. Tucked inside was most of the top sheet of a patchwork quilt I'd been working on for years. It was time to finish it. Or die trying. I had been assembling it over time, hand stitching every stitch. Very labour intensive. Very therapeutic, too. Jeremy had left a message. He had talked to his landlord, borrowed some money from God knows who, and made amends. He'd paid up through the next month, thereby giving him time to pull his belongings, his life, together. I missed him already. The stitch by stitch focus on the quilt would alleviate my diffuse focus.

I popped a tape into my player and settled on the bed, rediscovering the old pieces of cloth I'd long ago cut down to manageable scraps. I lost myself for hours in the task. Total absorption. I didn't hear the knocking on my door until it sounded like a jackhammer breaking through.

John Wilhelm stood grinning in the doorway. "Thought maybe you were in the shower or on the can," he said.

"What brings you knocking at this hour?"

"You want to go to a party?"

"It's Sunday night. I have to work tomorrow."

"So?"

"Well, I was . . ." I started, pointing to the sewing.

"You'll like it. Pick you up in twenty minutes," he said as he shut the door and left. I felt a bit put-upon, but not too much. My eyes were strained and my fingers full of puncture wounds from the needle, anyhow.

*****

A Village soiree is what it was. On the roof of a building on West Fourth Street. Colourful, tiny twinkling Christmas tree lights were strung about. Battery operated lamps irradiated the tar paper roofing and, most notably, the small, plastic wading pools that were set up. Lawn chairs and kitchen chairs encircled the pools so that merry-makers could kick off their shoes and dangle their feet in the water. Kegs were stationed in strategic points, as were wash tubs full of ice, sodas and bottles of wine. It was comfortable up on the roof. Cooler, pretty in a bizarre fashion, with a clear view of the lower half of Manhattan. Finally, after oh so long, I saw the wonder of this city, with its glistening buildings, stunning lights and incredible energy. My original vision, my original reason for coming here.

The crowd was divergent. Button down collars and starched crinoline petticoats attached to faux leather bustiers, Levi's and hamper rumpled T-shirts. Quite a mix. John was the type who could talk to anyone and everyone. I was more a wall flower, seeking those who seemed a bit detached from the whole shebang.

I found David and Daniel, very different identical twins. David was slim, with conservative attire and neat, tidy hair. Daniel was muscled, shaved down and into displaying his developed form. Long hair fell loose about his shoulders. Their faces, though, were identical, down to the small, faint moles on the left of their jaws, inches below the ear. Before and after shots any gym would be pleased to monopolise for advertisements. Jet black hair on both. Tawny skin. Dark blue eyes. David was straight. Daniel was gay. David was pursuing a career as an agent. He was a junior agent with one of the top players in show business. Daniel worked for the city, a maintenance grounds keeper in Central Park. David was engaged, his fiance another junior agent. They'd been together for four years. Daniel was single, forever in search of the right mountain of muscle and brains. Yet, through the evening, they never seemed to be more than a few yards from each other. David's the one who filled me in on their status as individuals.

"I suppose this is a typical question," I started.

David laughed and interrupted. "I always knew he was different. When Daniel told me he was gay, I said I'd already known."

"Then it is a typical question."

"Yes, especially since we're close. Most folks think we

should be bitter enemies. It's stupid."

"I was just curious. I've known some twins, but most of them were fraternal, sometimes wishing the other one didn't exist."

Again he laughed. "Dan and I only wished that on our birthday. People, relatives mostly, would often get us matching clothes or worse, a game or toy to share."

"Well, he's outgrown your size," I said.

David turned and studied his brother who was engrossed in a conversation with John Wilhelm and others. "He began that when we went away to college. He found outlets."

"Outlets?"

"Friends. Gay friends. He was a virgin until he was twenty. I tried to work out with him. He wanted me to look as good as he did. We're natural mesomorphs, but he thought we were too skinny. I'm happy with the way I am, right now at least."

"Until the fat creeps in for a permanent visit?" I said.

"Yeah," he said as we both turned to stare out at the view." Do you have a lover?"

"No," I said.

"Neither does Dan."

"You told me."

He looked at me with a wry smile. "I think I'd approve of you," he said. I let out such a guffaw, it startled him. "I meant that as a compliment."

I composed myself. "I know you did. I think that's the most flattering thing any well balanced person's ever said to me."

"Well?"

"Your brother is, literally, a cross between Tarzan and Adonis. While we might become friends, I know full well when to do a reality check."

"Selling both you and him kind of short, aren't you?"

"Have you ever seen him date someone like me? I mean physically built like me?"

He thought about it for a minute or two. "Not in a very long time." He seemed a bit surprised by the revelation.

"There's a lot about the nuance of gay subculture he's probably not made you aware of. I'm sure ninety-nine percent of his dates look a lot like him."

David nodded with a sigh. "So why's he not settled in with someone?"

"You want him to be?"

"Sure. There's too much going on out there with AIDS and all. I worry sometimes about losing him."

"He'll do right," I said surprised by the sound of my own conviction of an assessment of a complete stranger's character and judgement.

We decided to join Dan and John and their group. The boys introduced us to everyone, most importantly to Sylvia. She was an independent researcher, aiding film and theatre set designers and prop masters in finding correct pieces of furniture and bric-a-brac for their projects. I was immediately interested in her career. I'd gotten a degree in Theatre as an undergraduate. Props and set design were my forte. I had loved the creation of illusion of another place and time. She mentioned some problems with research materials she was hunting for a small production of *Hedda Gabler*. I'd done my final project on Ibsen's period. I still had the project, complete with sketches and photocopies and references locked away in one of my boxes. I couldn't understand why there was such a problem for her in unearthing the stuff. She said that pictures of rooms were scarce. Many old texts in the libraries had been stolen or lost or destroyed. Private libraries didn't allow her much access to their wares, if they did at all. I was about to offer her the material when she cut me off.

"How much do you want for it?"

"How much what?" I asked.

"Money," she said.

Money. I hadn't thought to sell it to her. John Wilhelm interceded. "You said earlier that you're getting too much work. Why not allow someone else entry into your business?" he said to Sylvia.

She pursed her lips in a rather sneerish fashion. "It took me years to get my contacts," she said. "I can't just give them away."

"They're gonna go find someone else if you can't deliver the goods," John said. "You appreciate people who appreciate the kind of work you do. Look over his stuff."

She cocked a brow at John Wilhelm. "And you've got a big enough mouth and know enough of the same people. Well, I suppose it wouldn't hurt to share a bit of the work." She then looked me square in the eye. "Mind you, I'm not attacking you, but I've spent a good number of years creating a job, if you will, that the business will think is indispensable. They're too busy or too lazy to want to do it themselves."

John slapped me on the shoulder. "Sylvia's shrewd. She created her own marketplace."

"Give me your address," I said. "I'll dig it up this week and mail you a copy."

She dug a business card out of her purse and handed it to me. "Dig it out by tomorrow. I want it by Thursday at the latest."

"I'll do that," I said. We made some more small talk, then Sylvia and some of the others left. It was getting very late. For whatever reason, David gave me his number and Dan's, with a comment to give him a call later in the week. I'd hoped he wasn't planning on trying to sell his brother on me. I wasn't ready to be forced into a date with a man who wasn't interested in dating me. Well, if it did happen, I'd let Dan off the hook with a movie and honesty.

John and I finally bade a good night to our hosts, whom I hadn't met the whole night long. John wanted to go to Limelight or The Saint. He felt like dancing. I was his only option for a partner at that hour. I said no. My mind wouldn't cope well with the thump-thump-thumping of the beat, so to speak. I didn't dance. Gave up dancing years ago. Gave it up along with the alcohol and the drugs. Clubs made me melancholy, remembering the past. Besides, I was rather suspect of just how he danced. I was sure that massive body of his flew around in some sort of trancelike ecstasy on a dance floor. Not that that would be bad or embarrassing, but I knew I didn't have that kind of energy. He let it go and went on to urge me to follow through with Sylvia.

*****

John and I separated in the hallway once again. I scrawled a note to myself to dig out the information Sylvia wanted and taped it to my front door. The message light on my answering machine was a steady ready glow. No one called.

*****

I copied all the material, seventy seven pages worth, while at work. I told Gerald about the offer that had been made to me. He encouraged me to go for it. Find some career path. He even gave me a list of his theatre contacts who were always pulling together very low budget productions. While there may not be a lot of money to be made with these people, he suggested that they'd be good for references if they liked the work I did.

*****

As with every other week, this one slipped along into the unmarked pages of history. I sent out the material to Sylvia on Monday. Tuesday I had tea with Peter and Paul and filled them in on the weekend. By Wednesday, I began to wonder if Jeremy had once again vanished. I had done my damndest not to get caught up in a morass of emotional subterfuge remembering and reliving making love with Jeremy, but I felt myself losing the battle. I declined another offer of another party from John Wilhelm. I was feeling tired. I crept into bed on Wednesday night, once again picking up my sewing and listening to music. I stitched and stitched until my fingers were numb, my shoulders burned with a dull, stabbing pain and my eyes lost all will to focus on anything. I cleared away the clutter, stretched like an old hound ready for his fortieth nap of the day, then slid deep into the bed to fall fast asleep.

Sleep didn't come. My mind was still. My body stretched again. I felt my shoulder and neck muscles pop. I hunkered down under the covers again. I could feel the darkness. Feel the solitude. I buried myself in the pillows, seeking some scent, but there was nothing. Our weekend tryst was no longer tangible. I turned over on my back, my eyes trying to open, but refusing to. Through narrow slits, I saw between real time and dream time. A vague, diffuse form of light was at the foot of the bed. Soft, quivering movements. Something was there, but not there. I felt my heart pounding steadily. I forced my eyes open and sat up slowly. There was no light. I'd drawn the blinds and the heavy curtains that I normally only closed in wintertime. A black void. That was all.

I flopped back, exhausted, and turned toward my clock. The neon red display was off. There was an obvious power failure. I fumbled out of bed to the window. The street was pitch black. I fished around in the blackness for my pants and pulled my watch with it's day-glo face and dial out of the pocket. 1:33 in the a.m. I set the watch on the nightstand and climbed back in bed, hoping to fall asleep and to not oversleep. As my eyelids fluttered closed once again, the image of light shimmered at the foot of my bed. I clamped my eyes shut tight and buried my head under the pillows. At one time, I'd longed for those little green men to come and steal me away through space, through time. Now . . . Now, I just wanted some sleep.

*****

Casey's face. A black and white negative free floating before me. She smiled pleasantly. Pivoted away. Jesus, Mohammed and Krishna, all laughing portraits huddled together. They dissipated into dark particles of ash set adrift on the water. Fuzzy ducks appeared, gobbling up the pieces of ash. The flock alighted, taking flight. Up. Into a gray, gray sky. Breaking through obscurity, the curtain of clouds pulled back revealing a form, a human form of light, standing on a small, crescent beach flanked by bleached white cliffs that stretched down to the shore like a mother's arms, cradling it. An apron of murky green water ebbed along the sand. Serene. Their radiant glow slowly spread its arms wide. It was a man. Some man. One of the three holy men? A life force come for a visit in my mind? Something from my own buried psyche seeking to emerge? The form held its arms out wide, as if waiting for me to walk into its embrace. In an instant, a rose bush germinated at its feet and rushed to full bloom. The cliffs blurred. The water withdrew. In another instant, the form and the rose bush blended as one brilliant beacon afloat in the desert. The sand slipped away at the edges of the image, the grains pouring out into oblivion; slipped away until all that was left was the radiating glow of the plant, its leaves, its blooms, its roots slowly spinning in space, collapsing into itself until there was nothing more than a crimson ball of light that suddenly shot like a bullet towards me.

I sat up abruptly, my heart pounding in my throat. I looked over instinctively at the clock. 12:00 blinked off and on, off and on, on the display. Daylight seeped in around the curtains. I looked at my watch. It was 5:35. I flopped back for a second,feeling completely drained. However, I knew if I didn't get up then, I would lapse back into slumber for too, too long. I sat on the edge of the bed and reset the clock. Arching my back in a stretch, I stood and shuffled to the tub room. Another day. Another further slip into oblivion.

*****

I drank pots of coffee at work, straining to keep my eyes open. It worked to a point. My body was fatigued, but my head buzzed with energy. Rather like being sick with a fever.

Somewhere around two o'clock I got a telephone call from Casey. She invited me to a picnic in the park that she and Michael were pulling together. He was heading out, back to California on Monday. I accepted the offer, as I typed yet another pointless memorandum for distribution to faculty that rarely even glanced at memos before tossing them in the trash. Five o'clock was very sluggish in coming. I practically bolted to the elevator one minute after the clock struck five.

*****

I stowed away my slim supply of groceries, mostly fruit and croissants, before playing the messages on the answering machine. Emma called. She wanted to meet with me. Visions of her jabbing a humongous piece of cutlery into my chest and stomach made me shiver. She wasn't first on my list to call back. I'd been stabbed once before. More like grazed, perhaps, but sliced nonetheless. Michael left me a message about the picnic. Sylvia called. She was impressed with my work. I could tell from the tone of her voice, she hadn't expected to be and was a bit disgruntled that she'd liked it. Carron called to see how I was doing. Jeremy called. Jeremy. A long message. He'd stopped by his agent's office and was sent on a call. He'd be gone for two weeks, to Cayman, to do a photo shoot. He'd call when he got back. I felt an ugly, noxious venom well up in me as I practically put my finger through the machine hitting the erase button. My whole body trembled with a rage, a frustration, a sorrow I'd not felt in years. I stood staring, glaring, at the answering machine for some time, taking deep, slow breaths to quell the compulsion to strike out. Logic and reason crept into my head. I was angry that he just up and left. Frustrated because I didn't want to feel so deeply connected to him. Sorrowful because I felt that our experience was through. He'd go on with his life and I would go on with mine. I was alone now. Alone again. I should be happy for him, I thought. He's getting another chance. I thought I'd had another chance with him. I'd known better. Knew that this was likely to happen. The previous weekend was just that, the previous weekend. We connected for a flicker in time. But what about his bruised, scratched face, I thought. Surely no amount of cover stick or other make-up could hide that blackened cheek. He wasn't a super model, worthy of such attention to detail.

I sat on the floor, absently toying with my shoe laces. Thinking. About him. Was this a lie? Why should I care if it was? I'd told him I expected nothing from him. He took me at my word. My fault. My feelings were my responsibility, not his. Be mature. Be adult. Adults go crazy, do insane things. Shriek and rant. Throw things. Collapse in tears. Call and leave pleading and/or hateful messages. Turn to stone. Stuff it down each time it happens. Keep stuffing it down, ignoring it until that day the box explodes and they go insane and take out a fast food restaurant with an M-16.

I sighed and sighed again. My stomach churned, coffee soaked acids eating through me. My mouth watered. I sprung up and dashed to the toilet, barely falling to my knees before the commode, and puked.

I fell back on my butt, my eyes watering, my stomach sore from retching. A gasp of a sob rose up, then turned to laughter. Was this love? Vomiting in the toilet? No. This was insanity once again come to pay me a visit. I cleaned the rim of the bowl with toilet paper, flushed away the telltale signs, brushed my teeth and washed my face. There was stuff to do.

I called Sylvia back. We ended up talking for over an hour, making an appointment to meet Friday at lunch to discuss plans for work for me. I then got back on the phone and called David. I invited him, his fiance and Dan to the picnic in the park. He was pleased, said he was sure that at least he would make it. I called John Wilhelm. He was out, but I left him a message about the picnic as well. Then I called Carron to say I had luck with her suggestion. She invited me up to her friend's house upstate for a mini-vacation. I said it'd take more than a month in the country to make me pro-active, but thanked her just the same. I hung up the telephone, tired but relaxed.

*****

John, Peter, Paul and I had jammed ourselves into the back

of a cab to get up to Central Park. We were all meeting somewhere around the boat pond. Peter and Paul came as they were curious about Daniel. My description of him intrigued them.

We found Michael, Casey and the others just setting up their space. We'd brought along a roasted chicken, an assortment of fruit, a round of bread and a two pound box of Godiva chocolates. Michael directed the proceedings, setting up all the food on one large sheet spread out on the grass.

John and the others got into some German dodge ball game played with a large, pink, squishy rubber ball. Peter and Paul fell in with Michael and some girl I'd never met before. I looked around. Casey was seated, motionless, under a tree. A small rectangle of cloth laid out before her with a large deck of cards on it. She finally looked up and nodded for me to come over. I crouched down.

"Sit," she said. I sat opposite her. "Close your eyes, take some cleansing breaths and let your mind relax." I did it. "Now pick up the cards, concentrate on a question and shuffle as many times as you feel necessary." I shuffled slowly, but my concentration shifted. I focused on nothing. I set down the cards. She split them into three stacks. "Restack them," she said. I did. She laid out a modification of a Celtic cross spread, the first card beneath the first and second card of the layout, all the while staring at me and talking. "Someone's looking for you, you know."

"A bill collector or aliens looking for a guinea pig," I said.

"Something odd happened recently at night?" she continued.

"I have weird dreams, if that's what you mean."

"Not a dream. Not really," she said as she looked at the cards. "I'll go through each card with you. Tell you what I see." She pointed to the very first card, the Ace of Wands. "This represents you, in a manner of speaking. A gift of creative energies. Tangible and intangible. Like the rebirth of fire from a spark. Expansive." She pointed to the card on top of it. "Ace of Cups. Gift of love . . . inspiration, imagination, nurturing . . ." She points to the card crossing it. "Conflicting that we have the Devil, which can be a sense of oppression, subjugation by others, or from yourself. Below that, your foundation, the Nine of Swords. Paralysis from nightmares or fears of the mind." She moved to the card to the left. "The Hierophant. The immediate past. A rigid, unflinching confrontation." She moved to the card to the right. "Ten of swords. Some see it as doom and gloom. I see it as an ending of pain with a new beginning on the horizon. Above it all, the King of Pentacles. Focus and direction and understanding necessary actions. Leading to the Magician down here. Power and ability. Above it, in your immediate sphere, is the Four of Cups. Feelings of uncertainty, disillusionment. However, above it is the Ten of Pentacles. Generosity and protection, if you will. The outcome is Temperance. Balance. Union." She fell silent for a moment, absorbing the images of the cards before her. "You have the power, the desire and the ability for growth, for change. You want to evolve, but you've been bogged down my fears, by old crap sifting in your head."

"Well, that's pretty true," I said.

"You didn't have a focused question, did you?"

"No."

"No matter," she said. "I'd like to tell you there's a lot of work coming your way, but I can't. This seems to me to be more of how you're evolving right now. There's a part of you closed off, refusing to open up to signs around you that you've the abilities to open up to possibilities."

"What kind of possibilities?"

"That's my point. If you have to ask, you're not seeing them," she said with a smile. She reached into my pocket and took a cigarette. I took one as well and lit hers, then mine. "Weird dreams, you say?"

I took a deep drag on the cigarette, exhaling slowly as I looked at the cards spread out before us. "So where's this generosity and protection you talked about?"

She let out a lazy plume of smoke. "Changes are happening for you, aren't they? Even small changes are still changes."

"I guess so," I said a bit begrudgingly.

"The Nine of Swords is a basic representation of fears. They're born from mental energies. They have no sound reason but you let them dictate your life for some time. You feel your ability to conquer them, but still fall a bit helpless and paralysed when something goes amiss. Like someone's out to sabotage your plans, to keep you from getting where you need to go."

"Well, yeah . . ." I started.

"You're your obstacle, I feel," she said. "For instance, what do you do with your 'weird dreams'? Ignore them?"

"Not really, but it takes me a long time it seems to get anything out of them, if I get anything at all."

"Like now," she said as she gathered up the cards. "I asked you about anything odd happening this past week. You didn't pursue the question. You didn't deny it either."

"So what's trying to get through to me?" I asked.

"Someone. Someone I feel you know," she said with a bit of puzzlement on her face.

"Like what? Like someone dead?"

"Could be. Could be someone who hasn't been around you in a very long time. Someone who needs you. You just got to be open when it happens."

"I have enough problems dealing with people in the here and now," I said. She continued to scrutinise my face. Studying every molecule, it seemed. "What? What's on my face?"

"A man," she said blandly. "Pale brown hair. Green eyes, I think. He's feeling sad. About you."

I found the whole notion a bit disconcerting to say the least. Wearing another man's face atop my own like a mask? How could I deign it credible? How could I not? For an instant, I felt that maybe some shadow of a past life, of a past self, may have been bleeding through. "How come I'm not conscious of . . . him?"

"You are. You're refusing to recognise it, though," she said softly as she stared intently at me, or him. Her face flushed. Her eyes lit up for only a fraction of a second, then she leaned back against the tree, a bit sullen. "He's gone."

"Thank God. It's bad enough having to concern yourself

with tangible parasites, even microscopic ones, let alone some free form thing from wherever."

Casey scowled at me. "You believe it," she said. "You believe it, but you're afraid of it. Your scepticism's hollow."

My mind reeled a bit. Pale brown hair and green eyes. It was my past. Him. Dead for many years now, a puffy, leathery, scraggly, decomposing body closed away in a box underground over three thousand miles from me. Him. Rex. I used to lock myself in on the anniversary of his birth and of his death and allow myself to feel. Twice a year for the first few years, I celebrated him by celebrating pain. Disemboweling pain. Suicidal pain. Memories as vivid as colours in a crayon box would assail me. That small part of me would never believe he was dead. There had been nothing tangible for me. No funeral, no viewing of his corpse. Just a headstone and a plot of land. I finally forced myself to write to the Hall of Records to obtain a copy of his death certificate. I still remembered the listed causes of death that resulted from the car wreck: Acute broncho-pneumonia and subdural hematoma, right, traumatic. Time continued, though, and the rituals evaporated. No one had touched me so deeply before him or after him, until Jeremy. If this was Rex's face shadowing my own, why was he feeling sadness about me?

Casey snubbed out her cigarette and continued to watch me. "The skeptic's melted," she said. "It makes some sense, doesn't it." She leaned toward me, intent on seeing, intent on listening.

"Why, though," I said. "Why now. Why not back then, when it was needed."

"What's going on now?"

"Nothing."

"Something's always happening. There is no 'nothing'."

I relented, but kept it short and to the point, recounting my shutdown after Rex and the recent repowering of emotions brought about by Jeremy. She sat up sharply when I finished my tale.

"What?" I asked.

"You know. It's a similar situation with Jeremy."

"Yes, I know that, but why's Rex popping in all of a sudden? Is he supposed to be some prophetic sign, or what?"

"Ask him."

We'd gotten somewhere and nowhere with all this, I thought. Michael, Peter and Paul suddenly plopped down with us. They all wanted to have their cards read. Casey obliged them. I gave her a subtle, understanding thank you and meandered off. I noticed David and Dan approaching the German dodge ball game. John Wilhelm hailed them. Dan immediately fell into the game while David tossed a wave and trotted up to me.

"Looks like things are in pretty full swing here," he said.

"I'm not agile enough for dodge ball," I said. "Besides being reticent to consciously make myself a target to be picked off."

"We came empty handed."

"There's way too much food as it is," I said."Your fiance didn't want to come?"

"Naw. She's got work she has to catch up on. The climb to the top, you know."

"Yeah," I said absently as I glanced at the game. Dan was already in the thick of it. "Your brother's no wall flower."

"He's hiding," David said. I didn't get it. He let out a smirk. "I told him that I thought he should look beyond long legs, big biceps and chiselled cheeks for a boyfriend."

"Ah . . ." I understood. "You didn't mention names, did you?"

"No. Well, yes. Yours was tossed in with some others we know."

"There's obscurity in numbers," I said. We strolled over to the food, he taking a banana, me taking an apple and a diet soda. "Except here, where I'm the only name mentioned that's evidently present."

"Sorry. I didn't think that far in advance."

"It's all right," I said. "Sculpted, muscled physiques intimidate me anyhow."

We absently walked on, toward the boat pond. Kids and

adults were playing with mini ships, sailing them around and around, getting no place specific but seeming to enjoy the trip nonetheless. We sat on the concrete lip of the pond.

"Dan's afraid of anyone not devoted to the body," he said as he chomped a bite of the fruit. "He told me he's afraid that if he's not with someone equally obsessed with working out, his body will slide into some sort of fleshy slag heap and before he knows it, he'll turn around and be forty and frumpy."

"There's truth in what he says," I said.

"That's ridiculous. We all age."

"Desirability, first and foremost, is in form among gay men. While there's always exceptions to that rule, we're pretty hung up on looking as good as possible."

"That's sort of like deluding yourself that you're gonna stay young forever."

"True."

"So why do it?"

"Why do women spend so much time with make-up and dieting? To keep themselves attractive. They want to be desired. Men look at the package first. Doesn't matter if it's a straight man looking at a woman or a gay man looking at another man."

"We're all gonna end up looking something like our grandparents anyhow," he said. "The sooner that's accepted, the sooner we all can get on with living."

"Let your brother do what he needs to do," I said. "He's sailing his own course."

"But he's really not happy. He's the type that needs to be with someone."

"Sounds a bit like you're worried he's going to try to cling to you," I said.

"Maybe it's me who clings to him," he said.

"Very shrewd and honest assessment," I said.

He smiled. "They're breaking up."

Indeed, they were breaking up. The game was disbanding and flushed, ravenous faces descended on the food. David and I pulled ourselves up and joined the swarm. Small talk was made by all before groups reformed. John

Wilhelm pulled Dan into the circle with me and David, leading us, somewhat, farther apart from the group.

"You guys shoulda joined the game," he said to me and David.

"We're targets everyday," David said with a laugh.

"Ah, but in this game at least you know what's intended to happen to you," Dan said.

"If you know the rules, you can play the game," I said. "Otherwise, you tend to flounder."

Awkward silence. John studied the three of us in an instant, then zeroed in on me and David. "So," he said, "Why're you doing this convoluted set up?" I blanched. David blanched. Even Dan blanched. John cocked an eye, knowing he hit the bullseye. "Well, you're not very subtle, ya know." David and I gawked at each other, embarrassed. Dan shuffled and rooted his toe in the grass.

"John . . ." I started with a cautionary tone.

"Hell," he said. "I already embarrassed you. Shoot an honest question. Make an honest statement in reply. What's so hard about that?" He turned to David. "You're the leader. Lead."

"It's all right," Dan said softly. He looked at David. "I know your heart's in the right place and I appreciate it, but you can't . . ." He grasped for words. "I don't necessarily want what you want for me."

David got the message. He shyly turned to me. "I'm sorry. I guess I stuck you both in a weird situation."

"Well, it's out in the open, now, so let's move it along,"I said.

Dan looked as if he felt guilty. "I trust my brother's judgement," he said to me. "Most of the time, anyway."

"My heart belongs elsewhere, too," I said.

Dan seemed to appreciate the easy let-off, though John Wilhelm seemed a bit surprised by this confession. He cocked another inquisitive eyebrow. "Who?" he pitched directly at me. All three of us shot him glares. He shrugged innocently. "Just a question," he said.

"Later, John," I said. He let it go. We meandered back to the gathering where we saw most of the people huddled around Casey. Peter and Paul came running up.

"She's phenomenal!" Paul said. "She hit everything about us on the nose." He took a second long look at Dan, obviously liking what he saw. "You should talk to her."

"Why?" Dan said.

"You just should."

"Take him over there," I said to David. "You both might be surprised."

He and Dan exchanged a 'what have we got to lose' shrug and grin. John led them away, leaving me with Peter and with Paul who was still studying Dan. He shook his head a bit forlornly and sighed. Peter was a bit unsettled by Paul's attention. Paul caught both Peter and I focused totally on him.

"Put your eyes back in their sockets," he said. "You'd think I was turkey vulture waiting for him to drop."

"Well aren't you," Peter said in a snit.

"The Meat Rack," he blurted out. "Years ago."

"What were you doing at the Meat Rack?" Peter started.

"Exploring depravity," Paul shot back. "Isn't that a bit of the pot calling the kettle beige?"

"Shouldn't that be the pot calling the kettle black?" I asked, hoping to stop a cat fight before it started.

"Beige is a neutral colour," he quipped.

"The Meat Rack?" Peter said.

"Oh, come on Peter . . ."

"You weren't virtuous either, Peter," I said. "Let him continue."

Peter relaxed a bit. Paul dove into dishing. "He wasn't as ripped up then, muscle-wise, that is, but he was completely ripped. Your friend Dan was into the leather scene. Bottom boy slave, even."

"Him?" Peter said, a bit incredulous.

"He looks like a lot of guys," I said.

"It was him." Paul was adamant. "They had that whole back area behind the bar," he continued. "It was a fuck bar. That guy, Dan, was a total raunch pig bottom boy, hoisted up in a sling Thursday, Friday and Saturday nights letting men do all sorts of vile things to him." Peter wasn't comfortable with this discussion. Paul caught on. "I didn't do him. I didn't do anyone there. It was too gross."

"But you watched?" Peter said.

"I was curious, for Chrissake! I was dating this creep who wanted to get me into that scene. I went there a few weekend nights the month I dated him," he confessed. "I finally got my wits back and dumped the schmuck."

"Well," I said, "That was then. We've all been around the block a few times."

"I'm willing to bet he's still into the scene," Paul said. "It's like an addiction."

"But, you don't know that for fact," I said.

"No," Peter agreed.

Paul shrugged. "Maybe. Maybe not. I just know what I saw back then for sure."

"Let's keep this to ourselves," I said. "Okay?"

"Fine," Paul said. "I just thought you should know, in case . . ."

"I'm not dating him," I said. "We'd just discerned that when you two came over."

"We're looking conspicuous standing here gawking at them," Peter said. He was right. We rejoined the group and nothing more was said.

*****

As the day wound down, I spent more time off alone with Casey. It was ego flattering to have someone focus so entirely on me as she did. We discussed dreams, expanding my own perceptive abilities, talking about my past with Rex, with Lisa and Carl. When I pressed her about her own life, she came back with a very, very focused description of past, present and the various approaches to the future she has the choice to take. She gave me a list of metaphysical type books that would lead me on my quest, stating that an open mind will forever be teacher and student. She cautioned that I could get caught up in the search itself. When studying theologies, science, metaphysics and anything else, let the flow of the course lead me.

Knowledge is cultivated. Sagacity, serenity, peace are the rewards of the quest.

We packed up around five o'clock, bidding good-byes and offering promises of remaining in contact with one another, knowing that few will be able to make good their promise. I was pulled aside by Dan while his brother and John said their adios.

"I really hope you weren't offended," he said.

"Dan," I said, "I wasn't really looking for a potential date with you. The notion was David's concoction."

"He does mean well."

"I know," I said.

"I'm . . . I'm . . .," he started with a frustrated strain. He looked off, combing back thick shocks of beautiful hair. "I'm more fucked up than he realises." I didn't say a word, just caught his gaze and drew his focus back to me. "If he really knew everything about my life, he'd freak."

"Are you afraid he'll reject you somehow if he found out whatever you've kept secret?"

"Don't you think there's some things better left unsaid?"

"At times, yes. At times, no," I said.

"Um . . ." he stammered, as if waiting for permission to speak.

I sensed his fear. "You want to talk some time? Without an audience around?"

"Well, your friend, Casey? She said I might find you a . . . 'receptive ear'." I smiled. Casey was putting me to work. "She's got a weird way of saying a lot without saying much," he said.

"You have my number?"

"She gave it to me."

"Ballsy, isn't she," I said.

"If it's a problem . . ."

"No, it's not. Maybe listening to you will help me with myself," I said.

He relaxed a bit and waved to his brother. "I'll call."

"If I'm not in, leave a message and a time and number to call you back, okay? Don't get cold feet."

He nodded with a hopeful smile and we parted, he

walking off with David and me wandering off with Peter, Paul and John to find our way home.

*****

The boys all wanted to go out to eat. I declined, wanting to be alone. My mind had kicked in on our cab ride back to the Village. I'd kind of committed myself to Dan. Who was I to listen to his pouring-out of pain? I wasn't a certified analyst. I hadn't even got it right with Jeremy, now I was going to take another person under my wing? I might do more damage than good. Still, I didn't have to say anything, I thought. That was my safety net. I could just listen to him, his secrets and let it all go, hoping the experience itself would help him. Maybe he'd be too fearful to call at all. Have second thoughts and think the wiser against it. Besides, I had enough on my plate, what with wearing my dead love's death mask on my face? Back in the old days, I could make my mind blotto with a quart of vodka and a Quaalude, lose all sensibility in a hedonistic bacchanal. An abundance of booze, pills and flesh eating orgasms. An image, painted by Paul, popped into view before me. Dan, fucked up on anything and everything, swinging lost in a sling as leather soaked crotches pounded his ass unrelentingly, caring not beyond their own base pleasures. The actions became more corrupt, more pointedly perverse as my imagination allowed the scenario to unfold. Chaps and vests and Levi's shredded to thread bare strings, coated in Lube and Vaseline, filled out by bodies. Skinny. Pumped up musculature with distended guts.Tight stomachs. Fleshy, fat forms. Smoothed by nature. Smoothed by razors. Hairy backs and buttocks protruding through openings. Stainless steel bicep bands. Steel cock rings and rawhide laces engorging loins with fever plagued blood. Cockheads swollen, sniffing for openings. Squirting jism. Shooting piss onto bodies, into mouths as insatiable bents licked dirty asses clean. Red hankies. Brown. Yellow and black. Fingers then fists then forearms stretching wide the unconscious boys in need of subjugation, of humiliation, of making their pains tangible to themselves, to others. Hard silver rods piercing beneath nipples, being tugged and pulled as biting brass clamps chomped down on erect tits with Pit Bull tenacity as studded, inflexible paddles slapped slapped slapped cheeks and chests, mutating all races into one scarlet brotherhood.

I felt myself aroused. That wasn't good. I shook the vision from my head. I'd never quite understood that scene in gay life. It was theatrical. Limits had fuzzy definitions. Total passivity. Total aggression. Was there pleasure in it for the passive one? Was it punishment self-inflicted? Was there something about transcending pain into a euphoria so extreme that it might be deemed spiritual? Or was there total self-loathing? I'd heard from those involved in it all that it could be everything; that it could be nothing. Better bonding though with a simple slave and master relationship than being what's termed as a pig bottom for any and everyone's use and abuse. Dan's secret. If Paul was correct, then I could understand him not wanting to share this aspect of his life with his brother. I shook the imagery and the second guessing from my head.

It was still relatively early. As I undressed, I found Casey's list of books and posted it on the refrigerator with a magnet to keep it from getting lost in the piles of loose papers that were dotted about. I took a sponge bath to wipe away the day's grit and grime then returned to the main room to shuffle through stacks of tapes, hoping to find some music that would fit my mood. Not being a music buff, my selection was very limited. For whatever reason, one of Blondie's albums was always selected. I popped in a tape and crawled up on the bed with my needle work.

I sewed for a couple of hours, replaying the same tape over and over until neither my eyes nor ears could take it anymore.I got up, stowed the quilting away, and took another sponge bath. Bored. Tired. It was Saturday night and here I was staring at my reflection in the mirror. I felt like I should be doing something other than letting hours slip by. I owed letters to friends and family back home. I hadn't returned Emma's phone call. The notion of calling still made me fearful. I could go to a film. Five bucks for a foreign double feature at the Thirteenth Street theatre. I could go sit on the stoop and wait for the boys to come home, passing the time people watching. I could shave down my whole body, but what for? I backed away from the mirror a bit, trying to see my whole upper body. The gym work was having an effect. Deltoids, pecs, traps, triceps were all looking fairly good. Still, the squishy sidecars known to most as love handles were annoying. Fuck it. I turned out the light, went to the kitchen, popped two over the counter sleeping tablets then turned out the lights and crawled into bed.

*****

I was mounted atop the mighty dragon, clinging to the emerald scales slicker than waxed glass that covered his long, arcing neck. We were flying through starless indigo twilight, out of the reach of time. He stretched out sharplyas he angled for descent with all the precision of a jet plane. I could feel myself sliding down, toward his head, slipping over it, then down his long snout like a child whizzing down a slide. I flew off into the void, somersaulting with panic, falling like a fleshy meteor toward midnight blue cliffs being ripped apart by turbulent black waters. The descent.

A crimson flash. The tip of his brilliant wing swept under me and flipped me up like a balloon gently tapped into the air then curled about me, holding fast as speed slowed to a feather fall. He brought me down and deposited me on pale blue sand as soft as talcum. With the grace of a hummingbird, the smiling beast settled on the sand near me, expelling a tired blast of peppermint breath, then nestled down to sleep.

I looked around. Deep, dark water covered the expansive horizon before me. High cliffs like so many giant shafts of fused crystal points loomed behind, to the sides of me. A cove. A quite, surreal cove canopied by an ebony sky and pale twin moons.

There was no place to go, save for trying to swim out into oblivion. My mighty dragon was sleeping soundly, his wet, glistening nostrils blowing little puffs of white clouds as he snorted exhalations into the sand. I stretched back into the fluffy grains and stared up into the sky. The twin moons slowly transformed into faces. Two out of focus passport photos floating high above me. I squeezed my eyes shut tight, hoping to clear away faint imagery. As I opened them, the moons had become one – one bright golden orb rising over the horizon. I sat up slowly, aware, yet unafraid. My reptilian steed still slumbered. I felt a warmth behind me. As I turned around, I caught sight of the rose bush, in full bloom. Fussing over the budding flowers were Jesus, Mohammed and Krishna. Each plucked a blossom, cupped it in his hands and looked straight into me proffering the beauty cradled between palms. I stood slowly and joined them, completing the circle around the rose bush.

"Beauty exists everywhere," said Krishna.

"Though only seen by those with the gift of sight," said Mohammed.

"Sight," said Jesus, "comes from within."

The three held out their hands. My own lifted slowly, with outstretched palms, accepting the offerings they poured forth. The flowers were radiant, fragrant, perfect. Each opened a little bit more. Then, from the centre of each, a bee crawled out, each dusted with golden pollen. The cold shiver of fright rippled up my spin.

"You fear their sting," said Mohammed.

"Stay calm and observe," said Krishna.

"Have no fear and they, too, will be unafraid," said Jesus.

I was paralysed watching the three bees flit lazily about from bloom to bloom. One floated down onto my thumb, its webish legs tracing a path over my skin in search of a payload. Finding nothing, it zoomed up, darted around my head then sped off. The other two followed suit. A warm flush of relief washed over me.

"Everything has its purpose," said Krishna.

"The universality of the equation perpetuates the cycle," said Mohammed.

"You may walk in fear no more," said Jesus.'

The roses darkened suddenly and crumbled to dust in my hands. Their remains sifted through my fingers like water through a sieve. I looked up at the trio. They just smiled gently, then vanished in a soft glow. The rose bush was gone. I turned to see my dragon standing, waiting to take me home. Before I knew it, I was once again high above reality on the back of the beast, soaring lazily through a cool damp night. I hugged my ride hard, absorbing the strength and warmth of his body, and slipped into a comfortable sleep.

*****

I awoke a bit rumdumb, the night's hallucination a fuzzy puzzle in my mind. The room was still, dark and quiet. I squinted to read the clock. 2:57 a.m. I felt myself let out a groan of a sigh, then rolled over and burrowed down into another sleep.

*****

I felt I'd slept through the rest of the summer. Months passed. I'd heard not a word from Jeremy. I'd never called back Emma. She never called me back, either. I'd been kept busy by Sylvia who threw more and more research work my way. Nights were spent leafing through books from the main library, from the University library, from bookstores, all obtained on weekends, researching everything from costume history to the history of welding. She was getting more work from independent film producers and their art directors. They paid her. She paid me, though at times getting a cheque from her was like pulling a fang from a pissed off cobra. She was cheap. She was greedy, always haggling on price and arguing over reimbursements for books that had to be bought. John Wilhelm and Julie of the saws had a brief August fling. John's detached demeanour didn't make Julie suicidal at all. If anything, she said, it made her appreciate the attentive passions of the woman she'd been involved with earlier that summer. I heard from David now and then. I went out to dinner with he and his fiance a few times. She was nice, like him. She loved her job. She even loved the political games that she had to play. They invited me and John Wilhelm to their wedding which was set to take place in February, on Valentine's Day. She picked the date, explaining that it was convenient to kill two birds with one stone. Get all the expected romantic days of the year said and done with all at once. As unromantic as they were, Peter and Paul turned into the opposite. They spoke with a counsellor at the Gay and Lesbian Community Services Centre and got over their issues of sex. Paul was insatiable, according to Peter. John Wilhelm and I hung out more and more during my free time, him dragging me to art shows and parties and introducing me to everyone on Manhattan's gray earth.

The dreams, the weird dreams, persisted sporadically, unexpectedly. Always the same cast of characters. I had started recording first impressions upon awakening, as had been dictated by Casey. I was understanding more about myself, about others, but not always accepting what seemed to be conclusions. Twice more something, maybe Rex, maybe my own imagination, tried to bleed through under cover of night. My visiting spectre. Just observing. I tried hard to see it fully, to see Rex's face as Casey had seen it on my own. I couldn't. Something in the dreams seemed to tell me that I still wasn't completely ready for a meeting like this. I had bought the books on Casey's list but had barely cracked the bindings on any of them. Then there was Dan. Dan and I met once, in early September. He wasn't ready to talk then, though he seemed to want to. The best he could do was to state that he had been into the underground leather scene for a very long time, had gotten out of it, but was still attracted to it. Our two hour plus conversation went all over the place. He wasn't sure what he was looking for out of life, save for gardening. He liked his job. He liked plants, tending to them, watching them undergo seasonal change, keeping them as healthy and as strong as they could be in the midst of Central Park. I let him steer the entire conversation, only piping up to crest the lulls that happened when he caught himself almost revealing himself with harsh honesty. I did my best to put him at ease, to be careful about being judgmental in any way. Still, his wall was too thick, too sturdy, too completely constructed for protection. I'd left him with an open invitation to call at any time. As yet, he hadn't accepted the offer.

*****

It was a beautiful October night. The air was clean and crisp as Carron V. and I meandered down Leroy Street, one of my favourite streets in the city, with its quaint, well kept townhouses on the north side and the old pool on the south side. Trees were alive with scarlet leaves waiting to fall. We'd just had a farewell dinner. She was going to England for four weeks. Sharkey was to be tended to by her upstate friend, given a month in the country. She was happy to take this trip but reticent to leave her family member behind.

"You can call her daily, you know," I said.

"Collect calls from Mom?"

"Quit worrying."

"I know she'll be all right. She's in capable hands."

"I envy you," I said. "I'd love to disappear for a while."

"Don't you have some vacation time coming?" she said. "You could take a courier flight to London and stay with me."

"I'm saving the time for Christmas to fly home."

"I should do that, but they want me to take all my time at once." They being her employer, an architectural firm with its fingers in half the projects in the city. We continued to walk and talk to the West Fourth Street stop. We parted at the subway entrance with a hug and a peck. She disappeared down into the bowels of the city to zip back up to the Upper West Side. I lingered for a time, thinking, then turned to the newsstand to pick up a paper. As I tucked the paper under my arm and turned, I spotted Jeremy getting out of a cab up near the old coffee shop on West Fourth. I trucked on ahead as he paid the driver and slammed the door. He started walking, briskly, east toward the park. I picked up my pace, determined to run smack dab into him and trip him up. I finally caught up to him as he crossed the street and stepped into the park, tagging him on the arm with a newsprint swat. He turned around. Surprise turned to a chagrin. He immediately embraced me with a jolly hug. I was the one now surprised. I'd figured on receiving a more hesitant response from him. He let me loose, then prodded me to walk with him.

"I was just gonna hike over to your place, only I wasn't sure you'd still be there," he said.

"Well . . .," I started. Just like no time had passed. I stopped dead in my tracks and whipped him around to face me. "Where the hell did you go? No word from you! Nothing! Now, you tell me you're on your way to my place? Come on, Jeremy."

He pulled back, a bit defensively. "I sent postcards!"

"I got one from the islands," I said, calming myself. "That was over two months ago."

He looked confused. He fumbled around for his wallet and withdrew a tiny scrap of paper. "I sent them to the same address," he said as he offered me the paper.

The paper was well worn. My building number was 107, but the seven on the paper was scrawled in felt pen. Sweat and wrinkling warped it some, making the scrawled seven look like it could have been a nine. "What's this address?" I asked, handing the scrap back to him.

"One-oh-nine."

I clucked a sigh. "I don't suppose any of the cards you sent had a return address?" He shook his head 'no.' I smiled. "There's no such number. I'm one-oh-seven. The next building's one-eleven."

"Yer kidding," he said as he took another look at the scrap.

"Sorry."

"I really sent you the postcards," he said with a sorrowful tone.

"I believe you," I said.

He balled up the paper and pitched it into a waste can. "Geez, I can't even get a simple address right."

I pushed him along and we continued our walk to my apartment. "Forgive me," I said. "I had just been concerned, that's all. So, if you were on your way to my place why'd you have the cab dump you out back there?"

"The meter'd hit seven bucks. I only had a ten spot," he said. "I should've taken the subway, but I didn't want to deal with the people right now."

"So where've you been?"

"I did the gig in Cayman. I wired some funds back to my friend in Washington Heights. He took his cut then paid my shithead landlord another two months rent. I'm collecting the rest of my junk this week, then giving him notice to find another sucker to bleed."

"That's the condensed version," I said.

"I took the left over money and flew back to Los Angeles to see my family an' kind of get my shit together. Started knockin' on old doors, ya know, seein' what's up with those folks I used to hang with."

"Trying to hustle a job?"

"Trying was the word. I had to get some money together. Real money. Not a couple hundred bucks." He fell into silence as we crossed Broadway.

"So, you were in L.A., hustling jobs . . ." I continued for him.

"It's kind of long," he said. He turned the conversation to me. What had I been doing and the like. Small talk to fill the void as we walked to my building. We continued this idle chatter all the way up and into my apartment. Coats were shucked and I made a pot of coffee as old habits resumed and he fell face first into my refrigerator, coming up with a cold hunk of teriyakied round steak between his teeth. He devoured the piece of meat as the coffee finished brewing. He washed his face and hands and rinsed his mouth in the kitchen sink then sipped the steaming cup of black liquid and nodded that we move off into the main room.

He seemed pleased to see that I'd acquired a real chair and ottoman. They were refugees from a moving sale across the street. Twenty bucks for both pieces. They cramped the space in the corner at the foot of the bed, nearest the windows, but they were comfortable and in good condition. He parked himself on the bed while I nestled in the chair with my feet up. He sipped his coffee, then set the mug on a magazine on the floor, pulled a small notebook from his pocket and flipped it to me. "That's what I've been doing," he said.

It was a passbook. A savings account passbook. In his name. There was over seven thousand dollars in the account. I looked at him, then again at the passbook. I tossed it back to him. "You've been working?"

He rested his chin on folded arms and stared at the floor. "Working. Yeah." He rolled onto his back and stared at the ceiling. "I made three loops, man."

"Loops?" I asked.

"You know loops?"

"Porn?"

"Fuck films. Two grand for each of the first two, then I conned'em into three for the last."

"Risky business, isn't it?"

"I guess," he sighed. "But I knew a woman who produced them. She'd offered me a gig before. First two I did for her company. Nothing special. Just being a flagpole for the lady stars."

"I heard most porn actors only do one a month."

"Hey," he said as he rolled back over and slurped down more coffee, "I needed the bucks."

"And the third?"

"Bi film. BI-ANNUAL, it was called. Stupid as fuck, but for a skin flick they had some high production values." He leaned on a bent elbow and looked at me. "They wanna use me some more. Producer said I could be a star."

"If you had to think about it, if you had to come all the

way back here to ask me my opinion, then that tells me you're not comfortable with it," I said carefully.

"You think I'm asking for your opinion?"

"Aren't you?" I said.

He let out a sigh and rolled onto his back again. "They'd be gay porn flicks. This producer guy, Everett, he does mostly gay films. The bi film was sorta like a test for him. See if it'll sell."

"But, you're not gay," I stated.

"What the fuck's gay, anyhow?"

"That's a question that's been debated for years."

He sat up on the edge of the bed and picked up his coffee. "I don't mind fucking with guys. I like fucking girls. It's all fucking sex."

"Would you be this reticent if they were straight flicks?"

"A little. Maybe," he said. He stepped over to the window and peered out. "It's just that most times I had sex, I was kind of fucked up on shit. A little tweaked or a lot cranked. Stayed straight through these though."

"So talk." He turned to me, sitting on the ottoman. "What's to consider?"

"Everything and nothing."

"There's AIDS . . ." I started.

"They're using rubbers. And I'd be a top."

"There's you," I said. "You, all of you, would be on video or film or both. Photo excerpts would be in skin magazines. Half the horny gay male population of any given city would recognise you when you're out and about."

"You seen any porn stars in your day to day?"

"Everyday. Almost. At my gym. There are three guys and a girl that work out at my gym. A few people gawk at them, but they don't say much except in whispers 'cause they don't want everyone knowing they watch porn."

He had a pained, unsure expression on his face as he toyed with a fingernail. "It's just that there was some shit there all the time. Coke, pot, poppers, shit like that. I didn't quite go back to N.A., but I've stayed clean the last few months."

"Or," I said. "You've got enough cash now to float you

for awhile."

"It'd be another thirty five hundred bucks. That'd really cushion me for awhile."

"Then do it," I said. "You've already done three. Your cock and butt are gonna be seen anyway."

He looked at me with a serious intensity. "You're not giving me permission to do it."

"Jeremy, I got no problem with porn. Some models, performers, whatever, are victims of that industry. Some are in it by choice. Lots of us have done the same without a camera behind us. To me it's all the same, but I can't give you permission to do something like this. It's your choice." He placed his hand on my ankle, sliding it under the cuff of my pant leg, gently massaging my shin and lower calf. I didn't move, just looked at him. "Are you interested in something?"

He slid his hand out, untied my shoelace, then set about retying it. "Well," he started, "I was wondering what's really been up with you."

"Me? I told you. Almost nothing."

He spread my legs, then slipped between them, reclining against the chair and flopping his head back, almost in my lap. "You're not seeing anyone, are you?"

"I told you. No."

He entwined his arms around my legs, studying them. "I thought about you a lot. I missed you."

My fingers gently combed through his hair. Longer. Shaggy. It looked nice. He rested his head back on the chair again, looking at me with mouth agape and sad eyes. "You left so . . . abruptly," I said. How perfectly recondite, I thought. This situation. "I'm tired of flotsam and jetsam, Jeremy."

"Is that how you see me?"

"Maybe it's how I see myself. Forever searching for something to float in and out of my life with a certain ease."

"What do you want?" he asked.

"Someone who's accessible," I said as I leaned back into the cushion. A fingertip whisked aside stray bangs matted to his forehead. A thumb craned around to softly stroke a brow. "Not poetry and rose petals and candle lit bath tubs, but friendship, availability, partnership, you know? I'm not that old, but I feel the weight of dozens of lifetimes of not getting it right. That's making me feel old."

"How do you know what's available if you don't give everything a shot?" he said.

Again, I felt that churn in my gut. That ballpeen hammer tapping at the corners of brickwork of internal masonry. That churn of excited nausea that makes one want to make love and hurl vomit into the toilet at one and the same time. He asked an honest question of me. My mind said to skirt the issue with analytical banter that would turn the question around to him, to expose himself, his needs, his wants to me. The words constricted my throat, but I finally up chucked the answer. "I don't know."

He scooted around gracefully, onto his knees, his arms digging under my thighs, squeezing them into his chest, his head coming to rest on my lap. "I'm willing to try," he said. "I'm tired of being alone."

I felt his weight bear down on me like a weary sigh. I stretched down, blanketing him. "I don't really understand love," I whispered, "but I believe I could all too easily fall in love with you. That scares the fuck out of me."

I felt him stir. Like a drawbridge, I pulled back as his face rose from my lap. "I'm accessible," he said. He slipped like a supple snake up into the chair with me, beside me. His eyes. In his eyes I saw Rex. Saw Rex's gentle face subtly smiling and nodding a heartfelt, warm, sincere approval. An instant. Only an instant. This was right. In this moment, this was right. I felt his fingers trace my cheek, down to my chin. The blind trying to see beyond what can't be seen. "If you reach for me . . ." he whispered as he pressed his lips against mine. I relented with a soft, pliable kiss. I pulled back slightly, seeing pure want in his eyes.

A lump rose high in my throat. My voice was raspy, choking down dissolving walls. "I'll do all that I can . . ." I said to him. We kissed again. Tentatively. Tenderly. He slipped back down onto the floor, his hands feeling, caressing my thighs and calves, as they made their way to my shoes. He removed my right shoe with the ease of a salesman, momentarily massaging the arch of my foot. Then the left shoe. As he pulled my socks off with one hand, he unbuttoned his shirt with the other. He brought my bare feet up to his chest, pressing against them. I could feel a heartbeat. His? Mine? I wasn't sure. He took my left foot and pressed hard, kneading the tissue skillfully. I felt a release of electric pain shoot through me, exploding out of me, then relaxation. He repeated the motion with my other foot. This time the charge drained me. Left me limp. Left me vulnerable. He gently set my feet aside, stood with hands outstretched, inviting me into him. Like a loose hair plucked up from the chair, I was pulled up by his strength. He removed my shirt, draped it on the ottoman, then nuzzled into me, pressing his face, his nose, into my skin, inhaling me slowly, deliberately. His slick tongue furrowed like a lazy plow under my pecs, coming to tease my nipples into attentive anticipation. As his lips came to suckle, my arms folded about him, pressing him hard into me. Velvety locks of his hair webbed my chest. His hands probed my ass cheeks, then swept around to my crotch, teasing me. I didn't feel my pants being loosened. Only felt them slide down my legs, then him easing me out of them altogether. His shirt flew off as he sunk to his knees and began his exploration again with his teeth grazing over cotton briefs, nibbling my erection. He wrapped his arms about my thighs, cupping my buttocks and turned me back to the bed, easing me down to sit on the edge. The jockey shorts slipped off. I felt the extreme, sharp sensation of his stubble scrape inside my thighs as he lapped my balls, then licked up the length of me and swallowed my cock in a flicker. Moist warmth turned to wet hotness as saliva flowed and his tongue and throat clamped down hard about my member like a greedy calf on an udder. Stomach muscles twitched sharply with a dull sting, forcing me to V-up and fold down over him, letting my hands flow down his back, flexed fingers seeking his ass. He let my dick slip from between his lips with a gasp, rubbing and rooting his face and tongue over my crotch. I reached under his arms and heaved him up on top of me, weaving my limbs about him like wanton ivy. I rolled us over. Him beneath me. His rigid cock strained against a layer of denim as I split the crack of my ass pressing back on his groin, grinding down hard on him. I slid up on onto his stomach and reached back, loosening his jeans, unzipping his fly. His hips bucked up a bit, allowing me room enough to slip the pants down to his thighs. I twisted around, turned around, shoved my face into his meaty bulge and pushed the jeans down further, riding them over his knees. He brought his legs up for me. As I leaned up to yank them off, I felt his prickly face push itself into my ass, biting, nipping, licking, tonguing. Into me. Nerves exploded as a wave of desire mushroomed through me. My face slammed into his crotch as eager fingers ripped through then shredded worn shorts, freeing him to snake into the den between my lips. My tongue probed beneath a sheath of foreskin, caressing the head of his cock, coaxing it to swell and stretch out, down my throat. He stifled a gasp. I let him free and turned to lay on top on him, my undulating hips gently rubbing my cock against his. He panted and strained to raise his head. My hand slipped around and guided him along to link his lips to mine. He grabbed fistfuls of my hair and pressed down hard. Lips fused, teeth knocked teeth as ravenous tongues drilled into each other. His hands pressed against my cheeks as we parted.

"You've a nice face," he said.

"Familiar face." My words echoed in my memory. "Like a horse."

He scooted over a bit, allowing me to slide off him and nestle into his side, burrowing myself up under his arm. A faint, musky scent. I liked his smell. What Emma found gross I found beautiful. His smell was him. Was male. Was security and reassurance. There was no part of him I would reject. My gaze traced a path down his torso to his penis, over the rise of his scrotum on down his legs to his feet as my hand trowled across his chest to latch onto his ribs, holding him fast there on the bed with me.

"You said," he started. A pause. "You said that you

could easily fall in love with me. Did you mean that?"

"Does that scare you?"

"A little."

"It scares me, too."

"A little because . . . Because, I . . ." he stammered.

"What?"

He cupped me under the chin and guided my eyes to meet his. "I don't know if I'm in love with you, but I do love you."

"You loved Emma, didn't you?" I felt it an honest question. Perhaps, though, one that didn't need to be asked. His eyes darted away from mine as if looking for a cue card to read. "I do," he said pointedly. "But, again, it's different. Different with you."

"Maybe . . ." I said as I shifted out flat beside him, searching for my own cue card. "Maybe we should leave that word out for the time being."

"Why?"

"The word alone can be a source of pleasure and of pain."

He let out a very slight but sad sounding sigh. I'd sighed as he did many times before. It was one of understanding the definitions of love and what they could translate into in a relationship. He scooped me into him and hunkered down to face me. "You're just as afraid of it as me."

"Love, the word, or love, the emotion?"

"Both."

"Weird, isn't it."

"Well," he said with a smile, "I think maybe you're right. For now."

Another kiss lead into complete, unconditional, fulfilment of love making. I was insatiable. Lips to cocks to asses to mouths to nipples to toes to ears to every cell bursting with pulsing desires being met again and again. Hours sweated by in a blur. For a second time since meeting, we soaked the bed through, falling asleep as early morning traffic began to flow just yards away outside.

*****

I awoke sprawled over a tangle of bedclothes. Semen and

sweat and lubricant perfumed the sheets. Fingers crawled then clenched fistfuls of fabric and drew the folds into my face. Heady. Heavy. I inhaled it all. A plop of something gloppy hit my spine. I jerked back only to be blocked by the flat of his strong palm as it pushed me back down on my stomach and glided up to my shoulder. Another plop. The other palm bore down. He gently kneaded, easily plowed over my back. I expelled an involuntary groan and fell to mush as his hands and fingers proved adroit at redefining relaxation. Deep pockets popped inside me like kernels of corn suddenly thrown into a smoking pan of crackling hot oil, each and every instance sending flashes of fuzzy black supernovas flaring before my eyes. More than my back, more than my neck, this manipulation of my hands and my feet so exorcised demons within that I found myself fading fast into another theta state. The blackness behind eyelids gave way to brilliant washes of colours, like a filmed perspective of an acid based mind trip. My lungs expanded like a newborn's, feeling like a newborn's the true experience of the air. His own steady breathing filtered in through sleepy ears as he moved effortlessly over my body again and again. The hazy veil cleared just a bit as he eased me over onto my back and began anew. Arms outstretched like Christ on the cross, he helped me discover the living being that lay beneath the shell of skin.

An oil trickled over me, all over me. My body was so much gelatin, incapable of moving if it had to. Then his fingers traced over me as I sensed him move around me, positioning himself above my head. More oil streamed down on my head, soaking my hair. Massaging fingertips spiralled through my hair, saturating it, invigorating me. A charged chill flew down my spin as my hands swept up to clasp his bare thighs. My eyes sprang open. His slickened palms skied down my neck, over the rise of my chest, across my stomach, then down my thighs, skidding around my swelling erection. His cock and balls come to hover a hair's width above my face. My hands found their way from outer thighs to inner thighs. A middle finger skunked out his opening and burrowed slowly into him, massaging his prostate. A tremble unlocked knees. He buckled with a sharp pant. I caught his foreskin between my lips, pinching it shut as it strained to stiffen. I pressed in him harder. His scrotum contracted a bit up into him as a dribble of piss escaped from his bladder and spurted down my throat. Warm. Slightly salty. Mildly bitter like unsweetened grapefruit. He pulled off me panting, with a panicky look of apology and reproach. A stray drop of urine dripped from the prepuce and found a target between my parted lips.

"I'm sorry . . ." he said hoarsely.

I sat up and spun around to face him, his cock. I swept oiled locks back then set a glistening palm on his quivering stomach. I stood slowly, sliding my slick hand between his legs then up, my finger finding his clenched opening. He eased himself. My finger slid back up into him as my free hand pressed behind his head and forced his lips to mine. As we kissed, I massaged deep inside him. Fevered breaths from him filled my lungs. His knees involuntarily buckled again and another spurt of piss struck my crotch, warming it, wetting it. I slipped my finger out, and gently rolled his member in my hand. An easy tug and a squeeze. I coaxed him, pulled him along to follow me. He seemed unsure but allowed me to lead him to the tub. We stepped inside. He watched me closely, anticipating instructions. None were given. I got down on my knees before him, my fingers again spidering up his legs. He slapped a hand against the wall for support as my fingers drilled inside him again. In a matter of moments a jetting stream of urine slammed against my face, my tongue, my chest, showering me completely. His body slumped with pleasurable relief and stifled, chopped groans. It was a baptism, for me. Inundated with human water. His cock stretched to accommodate his excitement. His hand gripped about it and jerked it spastically, jerked it hard. He almost collapsed as thick streamers of cum shot out, splattering against my chest, running in thick volcanic globs down slickened skin to my crotch. He flushed and gasped deeply as he sunk down slowly, finally coming to sit in the tub. A smile. He drew me to him for a final kiss.

I handed him the soap, then turned on the water. The shower washed all residue away as we lathered each other up and scrubbed each other down. If forever meant him, then I thought I could be content forever.

*****

We ran into the boys as we headed out for a bite to eat. There was only a slight instance of resistance between Jeremy, Peter and Paul, but John Wilhelm abated the tension with one of his usual, on the mark, honest commentaries.

"So the three of you got fucked up and fucked? That was then. This is now."

"Spoken rather bluntly," said Paul.

"Everything has its reason," said Peter. "We were actually coming to check up on you anyhow."

"On me?" I said.

Paul lit with a slight smile. "Thin walls, neighbour."

Jeremy suddenly paled, then flushed crimson as he let out a laugh. I even felt myself blush a bit. We invited them to come with us. Paul and Peter declined, stating that they were going to hit a movie with some uptown friends. John, however, had a couple of hours to kill before another one of his functions was to begin. I sensed Jeremy was a bit relieved that the others weren't coming along. Peter and Paul ducked back into the building as we continued on our way.'

*****

"So what's this mean?" said John Wilhelm as he crammed his final piece of toast into his mouth. "You guys gonna be a couple now?"

Jeremy nervously clinked his spoon in his coffee mug, sloshing brown swill on to the table. John Wilhelm automatically snagged napkins from the dispenser and blotted the mess, balled up the matted wad and dropped it onto his empty plate. Jeremy just watched him with a confused look on his face. I gave his thigh a squeeze to revive him. "Sorry," he said absently.

"What?" John said to him.

"The coffee . . ."

John shrugged, slurped down the last of his java and wiped his mouth. "My comment unhinged you some," he said.

Jeremy leaned back in his seat, thoughts racing in his head, across his eyes. "It just hit me," he said. "I've never been a 'couple'. I've barely been a single."

"Should always try everything at least once," he said.

Jeremy glanced at me, as if I were a walking abstraction. He quickly pulled money from his wallet and slapped it down on the table. "Come on . . ." John let out a minor guffaw as we abruptly slid out from the booth.

*****

28th Street. Chelsea. Near Sixth Avenue. The apartment was an illegal basement conversion. One of three units with arched transom windows up at ceiling level. Dark. Like a dungeon. A lamp with a crunched up shade sat on a plastic milk crate. Clothes were heaped in cardboard boxes. A futon covered by a down sleeping bag was near the door. A few books, a note pad or two, leather portfolios and loose tear sheets and modelling photos littered a corner. A beige desk phone with a cracked casing sat atop the answering machine on the floor. A pullman style kitchen barely separated from the dinky, dinky bathroom by a two by four frame covered with warped quarter inch plywood. Homey it wasn't. It was his place. Even John Wilhelm was a bit taken aback by the sight of it.

"Pretty gross, huh?" Jeremy said, more to himself than to us. What could we say, but nod an agreement." This is all I had to offer. Seen outhouses better than this."

"We could get most of it in a cab," I found myself saying.

John Wilhelm let out a bellow of a laugh and whacked me on the back. "A couple!"

Bewilderment. Jeremy scooped his fingers through his hair looking at John then staring at me. Anxiety welled up in me. A pitchfork was being tumbled dry in my stomach. I stepped toward Jeremy, unsure, unconscious even. "I'd like to give it a go, if you would," I said.

His eyes fluttered, his head pivoted to and fro absorbing the sight of his life laying about. "This . . ." he said. "This scares the shit out of me." This being us. Us trying to make something completely foreign work. My hand found his. He looked deep into my eyes, through them, way down into me. I could only shrug and answer with a faint nervous giggle.

*****

The first week was the oddest for me. He didn't bring much with him, just clothes, books and personal effects. The rest he left behind as a welcoming gift for the next poor soul stuck in that trap. It was odd because we spent any and all free time fulfiling very hedonistic, amorous needs, yet spoke little-to-nothing about our separate daily endeavours. Strangers, basically, who tuned it all out with sex.

The second, third and fourth weeks slipped by. The routine continued. I became adjusted to it. Me, waking early and readying for work. He slept soundly no matter what noise I made. He'd call me at work around ten and then again around two just to see how I was. I found myself having to work after-hours in Gerald's office to complete my work for Sylvia as I couldn't concentrate at home. Some of her contacts were beginning to call me directly, offering me paying gigs. I was excited by this, of course, but also a tad bit resentful as the responsibilities forced me to work longer hours. Yet, I'd always come home after three hours or so of extra work and at least an hour of gym time to find him waiting for me with a nice meal. He was becoming the hausfrau it seemed.

Thanksgiving was suddenly upon us. I came home from the gym that Wednesday before Turkey Day. I'd been invited upstate to Carron's friend's house. Carron, herself, took the liberty of personally including Jeremy via the telephone. In all the weeks, I still hadn't brought them together for a formal introduction. I hadn't introduced him to anyone outside of the building. He hadn't introduced me to his friends, either. That's why it didn't really surprise me that I didn't find him there that night. I took a slow walk through the apartment, noting that nothing of his was missing, save him. I felt a bit reassured, but still a bit uneasy as I had absolutely no idea where he might be. He'd been living, he said, off of the seven thousand dollars he'd saved from the skin flicks.

I was a bit annoyed with myself for wondering anything. I didn't own him. He had no ownership over me. That's the way it'd been. That's the way it should stay. I took a quick shower to wash away gym sweat, then grabbed a pear and watercrackers to nibble on as I waded through the mail, slicing even slivers of fruit with a small paring knife. I was going over the phone bill meticulously noting all the foreign numbers that I could only assume were his calls. Many of them. Long Island. New Jersey. When the telephone rang, it startled me so suddenly that I grazed the blade of the knife over the side of my palm. Capillaries continued to pump blood, completely clueless that the pipelines had been severed. I sucked red ooze as I jumped to snatch up the phone. It was David, of all people. He sounded strained, trying to control himself. He said that he realised it was late, but would I please accompany him to pick up his brother. I started to ask what, exactly, this was all about, but he cut me off, saying he'd swing by in a cab to get me, then hung up. I just stared vacantly at the receiver going 'annck-annck-annck' in my face. I felt the warmth of still trickling blood drip down my index finger.

*****

Brownish-red stickiness oozed through the wad of gauze wound around my hand. A slip-shod job I'd done of bandaging the cut. Thank God I never made it into medical school. I rewrapped and retied the sterile cheesecloth as we rode down Christopher Street. David hadn't said much. He apologised again then muttered something about wanting to 'run a sledgehammer' through his brother's thick skull. I thought about what Jeremy might think when he got home and found blotches of soupy red cells staining the table and sink. Would he identify it as blood and not pomegranate juice? Would he even notice it at all? Ah well, I'd call from a payphone and leave him a message. I glanced out into the night. We were approaching the pier area. John Wilhelm had brought me out here with those two artist women friends of his, M'greet and Susan.

"Where are we going?" I finally asked.

"Up another block, please," he said to the driver. "That building there on the right." The driver bounced the cab against the curb. David gave him a ten, then ripped a twenty dollar bill in half and thrust one piece at the driver. "The other half's yours if you wait for us. We won't be more than ten minutes."

The driver grumbled. "Gotta keep the meter going," he said as he snatched the bill.

"Fine," said David. "Drive in circles if you have to."

We got out of the car. I followed him to an unmarked door. The place was familiar to me, though I knew I'd never been inside. We went into the old warehouse and wound down a narrow corridor flanked by small, empty rooms. It was like a bathhouse, only much less appealing, much more roughly hewn, than any I'd ever been in. As we climbed some dark stairs, I could hear voices talking, could sense bright, artificial light seeping around. We hit the second floor and it became rather apparent that this abandoned structure was not so abandoned. A small film crew was set up in an old bar area. We walked right into the shooting of a film. A porn film.

There was Dan. Almost the way I'd imagined him that one night. Naked. On a steel mesh sling. Spaced out. Wet with what smelled like piss and cum. Some guy's fat, rawhide laced cock slapping his face. Another guy hovering over him, holding his ass cheeks apart while a rather ominous looking man rammed a massive, three foot, black dildo up into him. Other men were doing other things. Many things. A camera man was close on the dildo fed butt. Someone called out – "Who the fuck'er you?" – and David was in the middle of them all like a rabid mother badger out to defend her own. He kicked the camera from the camera man's hands, then knocked the ominous man aside. The dildo shot out of Dan's ass and bounced across the floor. Other men came at David, then stopped. He had in his trembling hand a fucking revolver. Like a cop's. The director came at him. He fired. This was no firecracker pop. The gun let out a loud blast that reverberated through the building. Everyone backed off. I came to my senses and went to Dan. He was large, muscular and fucking dead to the world. David was ranting, crazed with emotion. I whispered to the man with the laced cock to please help me. He did. We leaned Dan's weight on me. The man even slapped a towel about Dan's waist as we slowly shuffled to the stairs. Then, out of nowhere, another guy, very young, very innocent looking, naked save for a leather harness and studded, leather jock strap, slipped up under Dan's other shoulder. David glared at him, his gun still twitching around.

"Let's go," I said calmly.

"Our stuff . . ." the kid said. I took Dan's weight as David stared at him with tear streaked eyes. The kid snagged up a backpack and a gym bag, then helped me carry Dan out. We descended the stairs. I heard David shoot once more. Our pace picked up out of fear.

We burst through the door. The cab was still there. The driver seemed shocked, even disgusted as I dumped the kid and Dan into the cab. Before I knew it, David fell into the backseat with us and slammed the door. He silently handed the driver the other half of the twenty. The cabby spat out something about stinking up his cab, but David's crazed look shut him up.

*****

David and the kid were in the tub room with Dan, trying to

clean him up and revive him. I made coffee, trying to deafen my ears to David's ranting, pleading outbursts. My hand was throbbing. Jeremy still wasn't home. There wasn't any message from him. I felt nauseated.

The kid came out from the tub room, towelling his hair. The harness and jock strap were gone. He was naked. I poured him a mug of black coffee. He took it and sat at the tiny table, sipping it slowly as he stared at the wall. He was slight, agile looking, like a runner. Pale blue eyes and fine, shaggy blond hair. I left him to think, then went to the sink to rewash and re-bandage my cut. Blood stains were still on the counter. I was trying to knot the gauze with my free hand when his hands pushed my hand aside. He tied it for me.

"Thanks," I said.

"No problem." I finally looked straight at him. "I'm Adam."

"Hello, Adam," I said.

"Dan's brother's kind of . . ."

"Frantic?"

He nodded. "He told me you're a friend of theirs?" I nodded. "Fuckin' scene with the gun, man."

"You're not fucking kidding," I said. "Your stuff's there by the door."

He went to the backpack and pulled out some clothes. As he dressed, I heard David and Dan mumbling to each other. I peeked in on them. David, his clothes soaked through, sat on the floor, leaning against the tub, cradling his crying brother. He'd vomited. In the tub and out of it. Another normal, abnormal night.

I poured myself another cup of coffee as Jeremy came in. Adam was on the bed putting on his shoes and socks. A grin flashed on his face as Jeremy gawked at him. He said "Hey, dude," to him. Jeremy quickly shut the door as I stepped into the room.

"You know each other?" I asked.

"Sure," Adam said before Jeremy could shoosh him. "We've worked together."

"At the restaurant," Jeremy said quickly. I let out a scoff

of a chuckle.

"Restaurant?" said Adam.

"Do you have a bucket? Paper towels?" said David from the kitchen.

"I'll clean it up," I said. "You should just take him home."

"But it's all over the . . ." David started.

"I know," I said as I looked knowingly at Jeremy. "Would you excuse me? Adam can fill you in."

I found David some dry clothes to wear. I filled the bucket in the sink with soapy water, grabbed some old dish towels and went into the tub room with him. He was too preoccupied with Dan to worry about stripping down and changing in front of me. Didn't really matter. I mopped up vomit on and around the tub first, rinsing the rags in the tub. Dan was huddled naked in the corner, queasy, straining back into consciousness.

"I'm sorry about all this," David said.

"Did you shoot anyone?"

"No . . ." he said. "I wanted to. God, I wanted to."

I rinsed the tub with the bucket, then pulled a bottle of bleach from a corner supply box and filled the tub with Clorox and water. The smell was strong, but clean. I scrubbed the floor and tub again as David tried to revive Dan. Dan groaned and clutched his stomach. I snagged the bucket and shot it in front of him as he spewed forth more vomit. Mostly bile this time. His eyes teared, his nose ran. David wiped Dan's face with his shirt tail. My shirt tail. Weird. I dumped the bucket load down the toilet, then went to the closet to hunt for something that might fit Dan. It struck me that Adam had brought the bags.

I found Jeremy at the sink, staring at the bloodied counter. "What happened here?"

I held up my bleach soaked, stinging, bandaged hand. "Minor accident." I picked up the gym bag. Adam was staring out the window. Too much all at once for me. I took the bag into the tub room, dug out Dan's clothes then helped David dress him.

I helped David lug Dan out of the apartment, out of the

building. While waiting for a cab to pass, David again apologised and thanked me. I said that I really wanted Dan to call me. I thought enough had transpired tonight to allow him to put aside his fears and talk.

"I have to get him some real help," David said.

"Don't light into him," I said. "He's going to be scared of you right now."

A cab happened by. The brothers poured themselves into it and disappeared. It was late. Fucking late. I was exhausted. I'd call in sick tomorrow, I thought, then remembered that it was a holiday. Relief.

As I trudged up the stairs, then down the hall, I realised I'd left Jeremy and Adam alone. A slight twinge of jealousy, of fear, pinched me. They knew each other from work. Work. The equation seemed simplistic. The porn flick Jeremy had done. A sleepy eyed Peter peeked out of his apartment, inquiring about the noise. I apologised and said I'd explain it all to him later.

I entered the apartment to find Adam sorting through tapes. Another glance placed Jeremy in the kitchen, leaning on the counter, staring at the blood stains.

"He was on a lot of shit," Adam said softly.

"Well, most of it came out of him," I said. He looked at me, then toward Jeremy in the kitchen. Big sad pale eyes. Lonely eyes. I smiled meekly at him then went into the kitchen. I came up behind Jeremy and wrapped my arms around his waist. He stood, leaning back into me. He took my injured hand, caressed it, cradled it, massaged it. "Where were you?" I asked.

"Later. Okay?" he said as he turned to face me. My gut froze. Later was a word that connoted bad things to come. I let my arms drop to my sides, away from him. I poured another cup of coffee as he aborted his motion to address me again. Adam appeared in the doorway, watching us. Waiting. I looked at him. "Do you have an apartment?" I asked.

He nodded. "On Carmine," he said.

Jeremy let out some weird sound and ran into the toilet, slamming the door behind him. Adam was uneasy. He shuffled a bit, unsure of what to do with himself. "You okay?" I asked. He stifled a laugh-sob. Tears wanted to well up and fall, but he wouldn't let them. Instincts took over. I set the mug down and embraced him. He hugged me hard, burying his face in my shoulder. I held him because that's all I knew I could do at the moment. I needed a hug. He needed to be held.

He finally pulled away. "Dan's going to be okay, isn't he."

"I hope so."

"You're Jeremy's boyfriend?"

"Yeah," I said, though unsure at the moment.

He stared at me for a few seconds. Studied my face. A shrug. "Not quite what I pictured," he said.

"You worked with him on the film?" I asked.

He nodded. "*Dark Knights.*"

"Was that the bi film?"

Puzzlement. "Leather flick. Like the one tonight,"he said. "Did it three weeks ago."

"Oh yeah," I muttered, pretending to remember. "He mentioned me to you?"

Adam nodded. "We were getting ready for the cum shot. I asked him if he wanted to come home with me for the night. He said his boyfriend was waiting for him."

I shrugged it off, casually. "You need cab fare?"

"I'm gonna walk. It's not that far."

I nodded. He picked up his backpack as I escorted him to the door. We bid silent good-byes. I watched him disappear down the stairs, then locked myself in. It was almost two in the morning. Jeremy was still locked in the toilet. I stripped down and crawled into bed, fantasising about a life in the suburbs.

*****

Verdant grounds. I walked over manicured grass toward a cluster of forms. As I approached, the people took no notice of me. I tried to press through the many backs, to see what they were all gawking at and whispering about, but they were wedged so tightly together I couldn't pry them apart. I walked around and around them, circling like a buzzard. Out of nowhere, a body slipped from the ranks in front of me. It was Casey. She smiled sweetly and took my hand. I felt a tremor below my feet. I looked down. The body of my friendly beast rose like a bubble from a green tar pool. Grass blades fused into the glassy green scales as his spine rose and caught Casey and me up on his back. Mighty wings stretched over the unaware crowd and flapped. We floated up, over everything, into an azure sky warmed by white sunlight. I felt secure as we flew in a lazy, circular pattern. Finally, Casey nodded downward. I followed her gaze. We were suddenly hovering yards about the crowd. All too familiar faces. Jesus, Krishna, Mohammed, John, Peter, Paul, Carron, Michael, Julie, everyone . . . Everyone stood staring at Jeremy, on bent knees, trying to reach out to a bleeding jackal who's eyes were glazed with pain and fright; who bared saliva foamed fangs beneath twitching, growling canine lips. He slowly inched toward the animal. The growls grew louder. He stopped. The jackal whimpered between throaty snarls. I looked back at Casey, then felt my dragon tilt. I slipped from my mount and fell like a brick toward the beast below. In an instant, I fell into the wounded creature, absorbing him, becoming him, cowering back on my flanks, wild with fear. Blind as a rattlesnake molting and growing, I sensed his presence, coming at me. Aching teeth snapped again and again at shadowy forms. Hands clamped down about my jaw, muzzling me, easing me to lay on my side. The growls welled up, but their escape was choked off. My body trembled as the forms caved in about me, their many hands stroking, caressing, petting matted fur. Friendly hands. Caring hands. Healing hands. A gentle touch massaged a throbbing pastern, then paw. A whimper of a huff and I fell into dissolving consciousness.

*****

Gray haze lifted. My cut hand was in Jeremy's naked lap.

He was tracing around the wound with his fingertip. It tingled. I propped myself up. "I'm sorry," he said.

"About?"

"I should have told you."

"About doing more porn?"

"About everything," he said still studying my hand. "Does it hurt much?"

"Throbs a bit," I said. He scooted down on the bed, bringing my hand to rest on his chest. I finally felt it when he twisted it around my finger. A ring. I raised my hand to see the silver band. My pinky brushed against it a few times. I sat up, drawing my hand closer for inspection. I looked at him. He stared at the ceiling.

"I got it today," he said. "I wanted to give it to you tonight, but with all that going on, with Adam here, with . . . Hell, I dunno . . ."

I nestled into him, allowing my hand to rest on his chest again. "He said I wasn't quite what he'd pictured me to be." Jeremy looked puzzled. "Adam," I said.

He sighed to himself. "We did it in the film," he said.

"And?"

"The afternoon we finished, we did have sex at his apartment."

My fingers drummed on his chest. I should respond, I thought. But I didn't have a response. I wasn't the type to fall into hysterical fits of jealous shrieking. Normally, I'd just get up and walk away, but I lived here, with him. I couldn't walk away. He could leave, but I didn't really want that either. I flexed my fingers to stare at the brilliant bluish cast of the ring. "Silver belongs to the moon," I said.

"The moon is emotion, isn't it?"

"Very much so," I said.

"Then what is it you're feeling right now?"

"I can't say."

"Can't, or won't."

"When I came home tonight and you weren't here, I got a little scared," I said.

His arm swept about me, hugging me against him. He placed his hand deliberately on mine. "I had sex with

Adam in the film and after."

"You said that already."

"I did it because I wasn't sure," he said. "About what I wanted, or thought I wanted." He stroked the ring once. "Now, I am. I want to be with you."

That's what he'd said before, I thought. Then he was with Adam. Now he thinks he's sure. Was I sure? Would I ever know when I was sure about committing to him or to anyone? Still, he gave me a ring. I flashed on the dream I'd had. I was the jackal. He was trying to connect with me. I sighed. Yes, I wanted to be committed to him. Sex with Adam was sex with Adam. I might very well have done the same. I felt my fingers entwine with his. "This scares the fuck out of me," I said.

"I'm enrolling at CUNY," he said. City University of New York. "They'll take my old credits from college in L.A."

"What're you going to study?"

"Art therapy, I think. Psychology junk. The analysts in this town make seventy-five bucks an hour or better and get the whole month of August off."

"Clinical psychology requires a Ph.D.," I said.

"Then maybe I'll study acting and learn how not to be a shitty actor," he smiled. I snorted a snicker. He kissed me then curled up with me.

*****

We had Thanksgiving dinner with just ourselves. He'd found a market open that day and bought a small turkey. I'd always opposed candle lit dinners, dismissing them along with moonlight, love songs and other romantic rubbish. I changed my mind that night. It was romantic. It felt so alien, yet so good. We did a lot of confessing to each other that night, revealing the private black blemishes of our lives. He also told me that the films he did would be in video stores and porn shops by Christmas. Actually, while I wasn't completely happy about it, there was a piece of me that wanted to see them. To see him. I was sleeping with a porn stud. Kind of bizarre. Kind of erotic. Something for fantasies. I would be envied by some, I knew. Men who'd see him fucking another attractive guy, or guys, who would masturbate with their hands, with dildoes, wishing he were making it with them. An object of desire, He'd be. They'd spot him on the street and whisper to each other with lust filled sighs or would brashly approach him in a store, squeezing their own crotches to entice him to follow them to some abandoned waterfront building where they'd . . . I was going to make myself crazy, I thought. Stop now. It's done. They're done. He's given himself to me, not to them. Enjoy the meal. Enjoy his company. Enjoy him. And I did. Lovemaking surpassed every experience prior. We ascended beyond the plateau.

*****

Jeremy found a normal job again, bartending in a gay bar. He came out of the closet, so to speak. We were officially known in our small circles as a couple. A mismatch according to many, including David who thought I could do better. He was still hung up on the notion of me being with his brother. Dan and I had become fast friends. The intimacy of that encounter knocked all barriers down. I sort of escorted him to Alcoholics Anonymous, Narcotics Anonymous, as well as Sex and Love Addicts Anonymous, hoping he'd find some resolutions in one or any of the twelve-step programs. And he did, to some extent. I helped him by being his first sponsor for AA. I had been in AA for a small chunk of years before lapsing from the formality of meetings and finding other venues to continue to grow through. Dan found, of all things, church. He went to the Metropolitan Community Church, a non-denominational, gay church. He was getting better.

The Christmas season came. Christmas and Chanukah. Holiday parties, well-wishing shoppers and merry merchants. Jeremy and I booked flights leaving the same day, within an hour of each other. He, bound for Los Angeles. Me, bound for San Francisco. We exchanged gifts at Newark Airport. My plane left first. I boarded it reluctantly. I didn't want to be away from him during this first major holiday together, but I needed to see my family, needed to get out of New York for a time and needed to see if I could handle the separation.

Besides hating the expensive air fares, I loathed flying across country. I had no patience for it. After two hours of sitting, I was ready to run laps up and down the aisle. Cross country flights, nonstop flights, were only supposed to take, at most, six and a half hours. They always seemed to end up being ten hour ordeals. Twelve to fourteen if I counted the hours wasted waiting in terminals or sitting in a car or on a bus getting to my final destination. I smoked a few cigarettes, chewed wads of gum, watched a bad, bad movie, read a book, tried to sleep, but mostly thought about Jeremy. Thinking about him gave me an erection. Not something I wanted while being packed in an aisle seat in a jumbo jet.

I dug in the flight bag under the seat and pulled out his small gift. I'd gotten him an 18kt pinky ring inlaid with slivers of lapis. He gawked at it every time we passed the small crafts shop on West Fourth Street. He even tried it on once. It fit his right pinky. I jiggled the package.There was no noise. Nothing. I put the gift away and settled back for the last leg of the journey.

*****

He called me every morning. I called him every evening. He was enjoying himself, he said. I was too. I liked my family, most of them anyhow. We opened gifts on Christmas Eve, not Christmas morning. It was a tradition. Only children received Santa gifts on Christmas morning. The big gifts. There were no kids in my family, so I had Christmas morning free to call him. I had my gift in hand. He had his in hand as well. He was quite, quite happy with his gift. When I opened mine, I was a little confused. In the small box was a small, business size card. The script had been printed professionally. There was an address, a date and two times logged – December 31st at 7:00 pm, at 11:59 pm. I understood it was New Year's Eve. That's all I understood. When I pressed him, he just said not to worry about it. I'd understand it all then.

I thought about the cryptic message all day long. We were both flying home on the 27th. His flight would get in an hour before mine. I'd just have to wait and anticipate.

*****

It was a bit sad leaving home again, but I was glad I was sad. It meant that I truly liked my family. My roots. The flight was smooth and, for the first time in my cross country flying experience, on time. Five and a half hours. When I deplaned, I immediately looked around for him. He wasn't there. I went to the monitors to hunt down his flight number and gate. It was still logged. Delayed. Two hours. I had another hour to kill. Hell, I thought, it'd take that long for the luggage to be unloaded from my flight. I took advantage of the time to wash up in the lavatory and make myself as presentable as possible, then to make some calls.

I wasted over five dollars in change calling friends and getting nothing but their answering machines. I was mostly concerned with getting hold of Peter, Paul or John, just to make sure that our building was still standing. Whenever I'm on a trip, I tend to worry about my homestead. I'd once lived in an apartment building that had three fires in nine months.The largest fire happened when I was on vacation. Though it hadn't damaged my own unit, it was unnerving. This little piece of paranoia was difficult to shake completely. I tried to, though, by concentrating on Jeremy's gift to me. I'd carried the card in my shirt pocket, taking it out now and again to try to analyse what he was thinking, planning, when he had it made. The address was in the Village, on Ninth Street. I wasn't sure of the cross streets, though.

His plane finally arrived, another thirty minutes late. I swear he was the last person to deplane, looking tired and cranky and loaded down with stuff. He gave me a grin and a peck hello. I took one of his bags as we made our way to the baggage claim. Idle chit-chat about respective trips filled the time as I hunted through unclaimed luggage lined against the wall. I hoisted up my suitcase, it seemed heavier now, and we waddled out of the terminal. I stood outside, puffing on a cigarette, watching our junk as he went back into the claim area to wait for his stuff to arrive and to pick up our bus tickets to Port Authority. Two buses left for Manhattan before he returned.

*****

All the way back into the city, he kept dozing off while I talked. I finally gave up. From Port Authority, we took a cab all the back to the Village. By the time we got everything lugged up the flights of stairs and all secured inside the apartment, we were both ready to drop off for a nap. He stripped down and threw on a large T-shirt while I called my folks to let them know I was safely back in the clutches of urban decay. I took a quick shower before settling on the bed next to him. He was already in an open mouthed, drool enhanced, deep slumber. My curiosity would have to wait until later.

Later never came, though. He was tight lipped about the meaning behind the card. He'd just smile and tell me not to be so impatient and nosey. When I mentioned the issue to Peter and Paul they shrugged it off. This made me suspicious. Paul wasn't the type to let anything puzzling go uninvestigated. I then directly asked John Wilhelm if he knew anything about it. He just laughed a 'yes' and would say no more. If these three knew then others must have known. I called everyone, asked everyone about it. No answers.

Stupid. That's what I was. It finally dawned on me to go to the address on the card. I found the building. It was a well kept, converted, old townhouse between Fourth and Fifth Avenues. I knew I didn't know anyone who lived there. I walked up the stoop to the buzzers. None of the names were familiar, either. I stepped back down to the street and stared at the building. I finally gave up guessing and went back home.

That night we went out to dinner with the boys. Peter and Jeremy had found themselves taking a platonic liking to each other. Somewhere between forkfuls of hot turkey sandwich, I mentioned that I liked the building.

"What building?" said Peter.

"The one on Ninth," I said.

"It is nice," John said as he crammed his burger in his mouth.

"It's a little too yuppified for me," said Paul.

"Gentrification," said John Wilhelm.

"The East Village is the next to go," said Jeremy.

"They're gonna make it impossible for anyone to rent in this city unless they've got scads of cash," said Peter.

"There are pros and cons to every situation," said John Wilhelm.

I dropped my fork in my plate, cocked an eyebrow and shot off my mouth. "You know, I'm sick of you all side-stepping the issue."

Jeremy smiled his smile, tossing the others conspiratorial looks. "He hates surprises."

"You're goddamned right, I hate surprises," I shot back. "It's goddamned rude to play games, building up someone's expectations and anxiety like this. What if I don't like whatever the fuck's being planned? You'll expect me to be all fucking happy about it, then I get to burst your bubbles." I got up abruptly, yanked a ten spot from my pocket and pitched it on the table. "A good surprise is immediate," I spat as I left them.

I charged down the block, weaving around people, pissed off at myself for going off on them; pissed off at them for playing this game with me. I wasn't about to go back and make myself look like a bigger fool than I had already done, so I just walked and walked hell bent ahead to nowhere specific.

I found myself in Washington Square Park. People milled about, acrobats juggled and tumbled, musicians strummed notes, all of them oblivious to me. I absently bought a soft pretzel from a vendor and sat on a bench, picking at the doughy product and pitching bits of it to a few hungry pigeons. Darkness got darker. Time ticked away. I felt stupid, really stupid and childish. It was just that I didn't like to disappoint people who tried so hard to prolong planned surprises. I couldn't think of an instance in my life where such things ever met my expectations, even when I expected to be disappointed. I most disliked having to pretend excitement and jolliness and pleasure. The few times I let my true feelings be known, I was carped at about trouncing on other people's feelings, hurting them. "They tried so hard to plan this birthday party for you." "She searched forever for the jacket." "You should be thankful that anyone even gave a damn to do this for you." Blah blah blah. Well, I wasn't thankful. When something is pumped up out of proportion, it explodes back in someone's face. Mine. Theirs. Both. I felt someone sit down near me.

"You gonna sit out here all night?"

It was Jeremy. Solo. "It's a nice night."

"It's cold," he said.

"So? I'm on the icy side myself," I said. "Where did you pick up your radar? On Fourteenth Street?"

"They had a whole kit on sale. Installed it myself," he said.

"What are you expecting?"

I shrugged and leaned back, staring at the sketchy trees. "I've run everything through my mind from a toy train to an electronic black jack game," I said as I lit a cigarette. He reached over and took it from me. I lit another.

"Thanks," he said.

"Is this something you think I'll really like?"

"It's a gamble," he said.

"Are you going to be disappointed if I don't like it?"

"If you don't like all of it, yes," he said. "But life's a gamble, isn't it."

"All of it?" I asked.

"Got your curiosity piqued again?"

"Curiosity killed the cat."

He scooted beside me and took my hand. "Day after tomorrow,"he said. "It's supposed to snow."

"I like the snow."

"Come on. Let's go home."

*****

He slept soundly. I remained wide awake listening to his breathing and toying with the silver band on my finger. I felt bad for making a scene. Felt bad for making him feel the need to track me down. Yet, I felt good that he'd come to find me. I didn't tell him that simple action meant a great deal more to me than any surprise he could concoct. Especially when he said to come home. Five months had passed since he moved in. I finally felt that just maybe I belonged there.

*****

I stretched a lazy stretch. I liked being on vacation from everything, I thought as I noted the time. It was after eleven. Jeremy was gone. He was working today to stock the bar for New Year's Eve. He had easily traded his holiday shift for today's as the bartenders made a fortune in tips on raucous party nights.

I was annoyed that I'd wasted a full morning, but what the fuck. The rest was relaxing. I felt like shopping. Dangerous notion. I called my shopaholic friends to see who might be in the mood to hit the remains of the post Christmas sales at Macy's or Altman's. No one was around. Phooey.

*****

Thank God for credit cards. I went a bit insane in the stores. Everything was cut-throat cut-rate. Some shirts and shorts from Macy's. A pair of shoes from Altman's. Toys from F.A.O. Schwarz, some books to add to my collection, a new set of sheets. I was going to purchase a whole new set of dishes, but the box weighed more than I did. I piled it all into a cab and paid the seven bucks it cost to get me home.

John Wilhelm helped me carry it all upstairs. He'd been out front feeling the weather. It was cold. He said it would snow. There wasn't a cloud in the sky. When we got inside the apartment, I played the message on the machine. It was Jeremy. He was going to work that night. I wasn't thrilled about the news, but knew I'd have him to myself on New Year's Eve. John rooted through the F.A.O. Schwartz bag.

"Cool," he said as he pulled out a metal toy car.

"Isn't it? I love toy cars."

He picked up the bag and dumped out six more toy cars, various models, various sizes. "I guess you do."

"The doors open, the steering wheels and tires move on those two."

"What else did you get?"

"Shoes. Some shirts for Jeremy."

"Becoming domestic, are you?"

"What do you mean by that?"

"The gate on my wall?" he said. I flashed back to a conversation we had some time ago. "You're on your way to becoming that hausfrau you wanted to be."

"But not there yet," I said.

"Starting's half the battle."

"So, what're you doing tomorrow night?"

"This'n that."

"Some of your friends having parties?" I asked.

"Some. I've got another show opening at the end of January. Need to work on that."

"I thought maybe I'd call around and see what everyone's planned. It's kind of weird, but usually I get calls and invitations to at least a couple of gatherings."

"Peter and Paul are going out," he said. "They said they wanted to have a special night."

"My friend Carron always has something going on," I said as I rifled through my junk looking for my address book." Dan and David are probably doing something." I hated it when I misplaced things. I started sloshing piles of paper and paperbacks around helter skelter.

"I thought you wanted to spend the time with Jeremy," he said.

"I do. But, you never know. Besides, people expect calls and well wishing."

"You hungry?" he asked.

"You really enjoy eating, don't you?"

"Same as I enjoy breathing," he said. "Come on. Let's hit that new place on Broadway. The one with the home fried chicken and real mashed potatoes."

I was hungry and that new restaurant was supposed to have good, inexpensive food. John grabbed my coat and pushed me along out the door.

The wind came out of nowhere, blowing in thick clouds. John marvelled at them as we walked. I yanked a muffler from my pocket and bundled it about my neck and ears. He seemed to relish the cold, biting winds. They made my ears ring and nose sting. Finally we came in for a landing at the restaurant.

Tacky decor, but wonderful smells. John Wilhelm and I ordered the same thing. Fried chicken, mashed potatoes with white gravy, green beans and biscuits. Extraordinary food. I knew I had to bring Jeremy here. John agreed. We talked off and on between shovel loads of food. I tried once again to pry him about what he knew about my New Year's Eve surprise.

"Give it a rest," he said.

"I've tried."

"Last time you pushed it, you ended up having a snit fit."

"And I apologised, didn't I?"

"Shut up and eat," he said. I relented and changed the topic. "I think I want to move out of this city."

"To where?"

"Back to California. I miss it."

"You move back there, then you'll miss New York," he said.

"Maybe," I said. "Probably."

"Besides, maybe Jeremy doesn't want to leave."

"It was just a comment," I said.

He let it go. I let it go. He was right, though. Now there was more than myself to consider. Every big decision would require two votes.

*****

To alleviate my anxious curiosity, I spent the day of December 31st cleaning everything. The weather outside was biting cold with very, very dark clouds. Still, I trudged two loads to the vacant laundromat, came home and ironed it all, then scrubbed, polished and spit shined the entire apartment. I actually worked up a sweat. Jeremy had spent the bulk of the day at the bar. They had decided the night before to throw a beer bash starting at ten in the morning. Get their clientele in early and get them too drunk to leave. He said he'd be home by five. Somewhere between coating the oven with Easy-Off and pouring Draino down all the drains, I dashed out to the market. I had a reasonably light dinner of braised shark, rice pilaf and a spinach salad ready for him when he got home. I wasn't the best cook but this dinner turned out well. I even succumbed to romantic rubbish and lit some candles.

We ate slowly, talking about day to day things, then I cleared away the dishes. He helped me wash them and put them away. He seemed happy, yet a little bit distanced. By 6:15 he suggested we shower. I'd already had one, but what the hell. I loved to scrub him down. It aroused me. It aroused him. But, this shower was relatively quick, with limited eroticism.Time seemed to be an issue.

I was going to climb into my jeans. He thrust something at me I'd purchased on sale at the beginning of the summer yet had never worn. A suit. I'd had it fitted, bought a shirt and tie to go with it.

"What?" I said.

"Put it on, please," he said as he slipped on suit slacks himself. I hated suits. Never wore suits. Bought this one when, for a fleeting moment, I thought I should start dressing more grown up. I was going to argue, but decided against it. He'd never, ever asked me to dress any way other than how I chose to dress. I had to have him tie my tie for me as I'd completely forgotten how to do it. He helped me into my coat, smoothed me out, then smiled broadly, apparently pleased with the result. I also had a relatively new overcoat. Basic black. I'd loved the coat, but only worn it a couple of times. All dressed up like a kid going to his first communion. That's how I felt. I guess I looked pretty good, so long as I could stand perfectly still. He took me by the hand and pulled me out the door and onto the street where John Wilhelm had a cab waiting for us. I was hurried into the taxi and we sped off.

*****

We climbed the stairs of the Ninth Street building to the top floor. Apartment 5A. A scholarly looking gentleman greeted us and ushered us into his home. I was introduced to Miles Franklin. Polite greetings, then he pulled out some legal looking papers. As Jeremy signed on a dotted line, Miles smiled at me. Jeremy passed the sterling pen to me.

"What am I signing?" I asked.

"John said you'd question it," said Miles.

I looked at Miles, then at Jeremy. "I don't sign what I don't read," I said as I set down the pen.

Miles folded the document down, allowing me to read only the final lines beneath Jeremy's signature. He'd printed my name on a line that read, "Agreed to and Accepted By." Then below that it read, "Agreed to and Accepted By – Signature."

"Would you trust me," Jeremy said.

"Why can't I read it?"

"Why don't you take this with you, Jeremy," Miles said. "I think it's good that he has a mind of his own."

"Are you sure, Miles?"

Miles smiled and nodded then handed him a small envelope. "It's not a big deal." He escorted us to the door, stepping back a bit to take in the sight of us together. He sighed a very happy, yet sad sigh. "So much like we were. I wish you two all the best."

"I'll be back with it later," Jeremy said. "And, again, thank you."

"Go," said Miles. "There's a lifetime out there for you." Jeremy stepped toward Miles and embraced him. No more was said. He led me from the apartment and back out to the street. I instinctively reached for the paper tucked in his coat pocket. He caught my hand.

"Later," he said.

"Now," I said.

He grabbed me by the shoulders, forced me still, then stuck his face in mine and calmly said, "Later."

I let out an exasperated huff. I was about to shoot my mouth off when a gentle flurry of soft, white snowflakes hit my face. We both looked up. Snow. Soft, gentle snow was falling. Jeremy let out a joyful laugh and an excited jig. "Fuck . . ." I muttered. "John Wilhelm was right."

"Come on, come on!"

He dragged me along the street, heading west. We cut down Sixth Avenue for a few blocks, greeting New Year's revellers we passed along the way. I kept asking about Miles. Who was he? How'd you know him? Questions.

"So many questions," he said to me. "He's a wonderful older gentleman I met through John Wilhelm."

"What's he got to do with all this?"

"You'll see."

We walked some more. I knew the neighbourhood well. When we stepped onto Leroy Street, my spirits immediately lifted. We sat on the brickwork of the fence opposite the townhouses. "God,I love this street," I said.

"I know." He squeezed my hand tightly, then once again pulled me along. We walked up the steps of one home. He pulled out the envelope from Miles and took out some keys.

"What're you doing?"

"Miles owns this house."

We went in.

*****

Grand. That was the only word that came to mind. The

place was simply grand. Jeremy removed dropcloths, unveiling beautiful antiques. Some were well worn. Even tattered and scraped, the few pieces were elegant.

We ascended the stairs, exploring the old jewel. There was nothing I didn't like. Finally we entered the master-suite. It was the entire top floor. The cherrywood sleigh bed was freshly made and the covers turned down. A silver bucket of sparkling cider and two fluted glasses sat on the nightstand. I was a bit dumbstruck as it soaked in. I sat down at the desk. The delicate scent hit me. White roses. Budding in a porcelain vase. I looked at Jeremy.

"For tonight?" I said.

He nodded. I flew into his arms, overwhelmed by a flood of emotions that came crashing through my masonry. Once again, Jericho fell inside me. Jeremy eased me off of him, then slipped my address book from his pocket and into my hands.

"I had to borrow this," he said.

"Why?"

He removed my coat, then his, tossing them onto a chair. He straightened my tie for me, then combed his fingers through my hair. "Snow's wetted you down."

"I can't believe that that man would just give you his house for the night."

"Thank John. He told Miles about us. I met him about two months ago when he and John came to the bar for a drink." He looked around the room, then pulled a framed picture from the desk drawer. "He brought this down to show me."

I took the picture. A weird sensation filtered through me as I stared at it. Black and white. Old. Probably the early 1940s. Two young men stood smiling, affectionately hanging on each other. They looked quite a bit like Jeremy and me. "Whoa . . ." I said.

Jeremy took the picture and put it back. "That was Miles and his lover, Charles. They bought this house. They lived here until Charles died eleven years ago. Miles wouldn't sell the place, but he couldn't live here, so he purchased the apartment he's in now over on Ninth." Jeremy fished in his coat pocket for the papers. "This," he said. "This is a lease. For this house. A ten year lease."

I was incredulous. "We can't afford this!"

"He owns the house outright. The rent's the same as we're paying now."

"Is he crazy?" I said, trying to find the scam behind the deal.

Jeremy sat me on the bed. "He's doing it for himself as much as for us. He wants life in this house again. It was John Wilhelm who told him about your love for this street. Not me. It was John Wilhelm who showed Miles your picture."

"What picture?"

Jeremy was puzzled. "This one . . ." He pulled out his wallet and withdrew a somewhat warped, trimmed down photo of me sitting in Alice's lap. I'd forgotten he'd even taken those pictures of me in Central Park.

"He never showed these to me," I said.

Jeremy carefully stowed the print away in his wallet. "John never mentioned Miles to you?" he asked.

"Never."

"Miles is his great uncle."

"I'm a little confused here."

"Miles is his great uncle. Miles and his lover bought this house because Charles loved this street."

"You look a bit like Miles and I look a bit like Charles,"I said.

"They were happy here. He simply wants to give us a good start in life." He handed me the lease. "I'm going downstairs.You sit here and read through this."

He left. I tried to stretch out on the bed, but the suit came to mind. I went to the desk, turned on the lamp and read through the document. The lease was very simple. Easily understood without a law degree. Attached to the back of it was a letter to Jeremy and to me, from Miles. In it he explained that this gift wasn't being given to us because of ghostly appearances but because he'd wanted to share this home with another young couple who'd appreciate it as he and Charles had. John felt it was right that he pass it along to us. He trusted John's judgement and approval. John would be legal heir to this property and wanted us to be in it, to be happy.

I found a pen in the drawer. I took another long, hard look at the framed photo of Miles and Charles. Happy then. Happy to the end. I signed the document.

I heard the front door shut. Footsteps shuffled. I put the papers back into Jeremy's coat pocket, then went downstairs. In the middle of the living room, nay front parlour, everyone stood with gifts. John, Peter, Paul, Carron, Casey, Julie of the saws, Dan, David and his fiance, everyone in my address book who was in town and everyone Jeremy knew around. Quite an eclectic crowd. Jeremy came out from the kitchen, wheeling a tea cart loaded down with spirits and foods. People swept around, meeting, greeting, talking, enjoying the time. I fell into John Wilhelm's big arms and gave him a kiss. He let out one of his wonderful, obnoxious, snorting laughs and hugged me hard.

"You know what you're getting for a housewarming present?"he asked.'

"This is quite enough," I said.

He shook his head. "It'll add a certain look to the old place." He reached behind the old divan and pulled out his gate. It was my turn to let out a laugh.

*****

The next few hours were beyond great. Nothing could've topped it all. At 11:50, everyone got antsy and anxious. It was almost New Year's Day. A young man, one of Jeremy's friends, stepped before the hearth. The guests clustered around. Jeremy yanked me along and planted me next to him, between the man and the other guests. They were all staring at us, smiling at us.

The young man cleared his throat. He pulled out a small book, opened it and began to read aloud. It took a moment before it all sunk in through my dense, thick skull. He was reciting. Words for traditional wedding ceremonies. I was completely taken aback. My ears fell blind and my eyes fell deaf. Carron had stepped up beside me. John had stepped up beside Jeremy. I felt my knees turn to jelly. Carron and Jeremy caught me and righted me. The young man continued to read. Then it came. Carron slipped a ring from her middle finger and pressed it into my palm. Jeremy pulled a ring from his pocket. He said, "I do." The young man repeated some words to me. In the distance, I only faintly heard the old anniversary clock chime the bewitching hour. I only faintly heard myself say, "I do."

Midnight. We had married. Though not sanctified by church or state, we had married in the presence of witnesses. I'd committed myself to this young man and he to me. The rest of that evening, of that event, was a blur. The fog lifted as Jeremy and I consummated this new partnership with intense, passionate, spiritual lovemaking. Dawn peeked into the room as we fell asleep.

My mighty dragon stared at me at the edge of the shoreline. He smiled contentedly as brilliant rays of sunlight reflected off his emerald scales and bathed me with a faint, green glow of healing warmth. From both sides of the cove, they came. Jesus, Krishna and Mohammed led the way. They all smiled at me, then climbed up wings as red as embers to mount the beast. John, Peter, Paul, Carron, Casey, Dan, David . . . everyone – sat perched on the dragon's spine. I heard a howl. A happy howl. The jackal came from behind, his snout brushing against my palm. He licked my hand, then ran to join the others. Jeremy came to stand beside me. As confident and sturdy as a caryatid. Finally, he came. It was time to put him to rest. Rex, my first great love, had arisen like a phoenix to join the others as they departed from my dreams. Forever.

Also Available

Packing It In
David Rees

This collection of essays, written and arranged to form a year long diary, opens with an all too brief visit to Australia, continues with a tour of New Zealand and a final visit to a much loved San Francisco, before returning to familiar Europe (Barcelona, Belgium Rome) and new perspectives on the recently liberated Eastern Bloc countries (highly individual observations of Moscow, St Petersburg, Odessa and Kiev). Written from the distinctive and idiosyncratic point of view of a singular gay man, this is a book filled with acute and sometimes acerbic views, written with a style that is at once easily conversational and utterly compelling.

'Rees achieves what should be the first aim of any travel writer, to make you regret you haven't seen what he has seen . . .'

Gay Times

ISBN 1-873741-07-3
£6.99

Heroes Are Hard to Find

Sebastian Beaumont

A compelling, sometimes comic, sometimes almost unbearably moving novel about sexual infatuation, infidelity and deceit. It is also about disability, death and the joy of living.

'Highly recommended. . .' — *Brighton Evening Argus*

'I cheered, felt proud and cried aloud (yes, real tears not stifled sobs) as the plot and the people became real to me . . .'
All Points North

ISBN 1-873741-08-1
£7.50

Ravens Brood
E F Benson

The latest in our highly successful series of reprints of novels by E F Benson dates from 1934 and was almost the last novel he wrote. After *Ravens Brood,* he published only two more novels, *Lucia's Progress* (1935) and *Trouble for Lucia* (1939). By 1940, this most quintessential of Edwardian writers was dead, leaving a legacy of at least one hundred books – destined for seeming oblivion. The 'rediscovery' in the 1960s of the 'Mapp and Lucia' novels was the slow beginning of a revival of interest in Benson's work – which has subsequently produced biographies and family studies and two societies dedicated to his memory.

But *Ravens Brood* is quite unique in the Benson canon, a novel utterly unlike anything he had written before or would ever write again. 'It bristles with sexuality from the moment we meet John Pentreath, farmer and religious bigot, at his Cornish farm near Penzance,' Geoffrey Palmer and Noel Lloyd wrote in their invaluable *E F Benson: As He Was*. 'In the first thirty pages there are references to fertility rituals phallic symbols, lustful boilings in the blood, trollops, shrews, whores and harlots, a cockney strumpet, witchcraft, lascivious leers, a menopausal false pregnancy, and all seasoned with a touch of blasphemy.' The book includes, too, the character of Willie Polhaven (the name is ripe with innuendo) – perhaps the most overtly homosexual of Benson's gallery of ambiguous young men. *Ravens Brood* is atmospheric and outrageous: a rollicking good read.

ISBN 1-873741-09-X
£7.50

The Learning of Paul O'Neill

Graeme Woolaston

The Learning of Paul O'Neill follows the eponymous hero over nearly thirty years – from adolescence in Scotland in the mid-sixties to life in a South Coast seaside resort in the seventies and eighties and a return to a vibrant Glasgow in the early nineties. As the novel begins, fifteen-year-old Paul is learning fast about sexuality as his Scottish village childhood disintegrates around him. After many years in England, he returns to Scotland trying to come to terms with the sudden death of his lover. His return brings him face-to-face with the continuing effects of adolescent experiences he thought he had put behind him. And his involvement with an ambiguous, handsome married but bisexual man raises new questions about the shape of Paul's life as he arrives at the threshold of middle-age. This is an adult novel about gay experience and aspects of sexuality which some may find shocking but which are written about with an honesty that is as refreshing as it is frank.

ISBN 1-873741-12-X
£7.50

Unreal City
Neil Powell

One week in a hot August, towards the end of the twentieth century, the lives of four men overlap and entangle, leaving three of them permanently uprooted and changed. *Unreal City* is their story, told at different times and from their various points of view. Set partly in a London nourished by its cultural past but oppressed by its political present, and partly in coastal East Anglia, it is also the story of two older men – an elderly, long silent novelist and his retired publisher – whose past friendship and subsequent bitterness cast unexpected shadows over the four main characters. *Unreal City* is about love and loyalty, paranoia and violence, the tension of urban gay life in the century's last decade but it is about much else too: the death of cities; the pubs of Suffolk; the streets of London, and the Underground – in more than one sense; Shakespeare's *Troilus and Cressida*; the consolation of music; the colour of tomatoes, and the North Sea. It is a richly allusive, intricately patterned, and at times very funny novel.

'Unreal City is brilliant, understated, but powerful and should have a wide-appeal ' — *Time Out*
'Excellent. I suggest you buy it immediately.' — *Gay Times*
'An excellent, extremely satisfying novel.' — *The Pink Paper*

ISBN 1-873741-04-9
£6.99

Vale of Tears: A problem shared

Peter Burton & Richard Smith

Culled from ten years of *Gay Times's* popular Vale of Tears problem page, this book, arranged problem-by-problem in an alphabetical sequence, is written in question and answer format and covers a wide range of subjects.

Problems with a lover? Who does the dishes? Interested in infantilism? Why is his sex drive lower than yours? Aids fears? Meeting the family? How to survive Christmas? Suffering from body odours? Piles? Crabs? Penis too small? Foreskin too tight? Trying to get rid of a lover?

Vale of Tears has some of the answers – and many more. Although highly entertaining and sometimes downright humorous, this compilation is very much a practical handbook which should find a place on the shelves of all gay men.

'An indispensable guide to life's problems big or small . . .'
Capital Gay

ISBN 1-873741-05-7
£6.99